# About the Author

Halide Salam was born in West Bengal, India, but spent her early life in East Pakistan, now Bangladesh. In 1971, she came to the United States as a young refugee to escape the Pakistan Army invasion, which ultimately led to the Bangladesh Liberation War. Halide received her MA in painting from New Mexico Highlands University, NM holds a Ph.D. in Fine Arts from Texas Tech University. TX. She studied sacred geometry and art traditions under the renowned British geometer Keith Critchlow. As a visual naturalist, her paintings are Trans-Stations of Migration, Light, Time, and Place. Halide has exhibited and lectured both nationally and internationally, won awards, and participated in residencies in the USA and abroad. Her first book, Between Two Spaces: Reflections on the Spiritual Art was nominated for the USA 2008 National Book Award in Nonfiction. When the River Meets the Sea is her first novel.

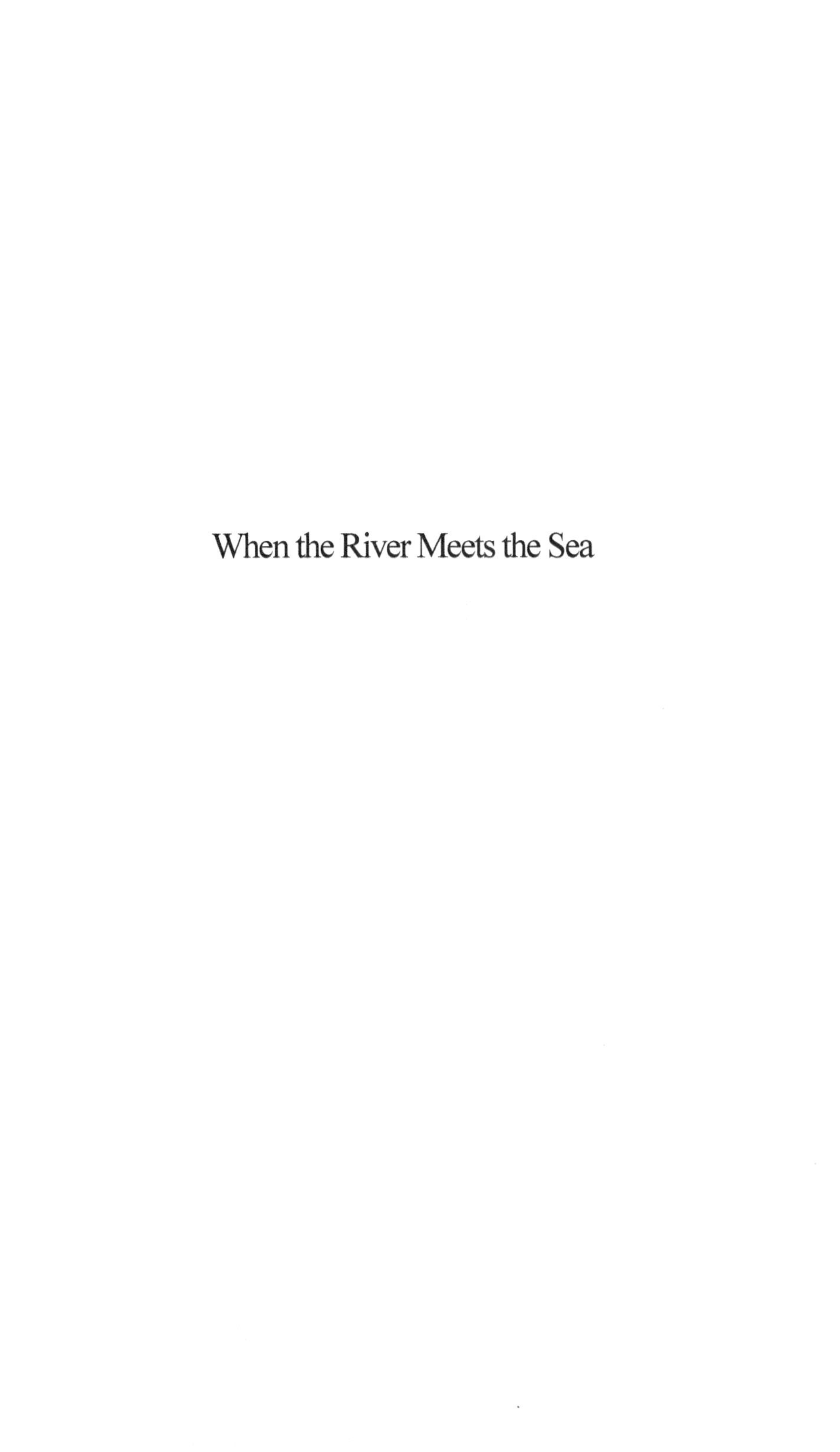

When the River Meets the Sea

Halide Salam

# When the River Meets the Sea

Vanguard Press

VANGUARD PAPERBACK



A CIP catalogue record for this title is available from the British Library.

ISBN 978-1-83671-020-2



*Vanguard Press is an imprint of*
*Pegasus Elliot Mackenzie Publishers Ltd.*
www.pegasuspublishers.com

First Published in 2025

**Vanguard Press**
**Sheraton House Castle Park**
**Cambridge England**

# Dedication

To all immigrants and refugees who weathered the
storms of their environments.

# Acknowledgments

All Praise to The Hand that Guides.

This story was written with the encouragement of my friends—Angela, Kate, Linda, Mike and Trudy. A special thanks to Trudy for her time and friendship.

This story is set in 1971 East Pakistan.

East Pakistan attained independence from Pakistan on December 17, 1971, to become the independent country of Bangladesh—the land of the Bangla people. The British referred to the Bangla language as Bengali and the people as Bengalis. However, since the formation of Bangladesh, the language reverted to its original name, Bangla, and the people to Bangali people. Bengali and Bangla are used interchangeably.

# When the River Meets the Sea

Being a *dou nas laa*[1] has haunted me my whole life. I was twelve when I first heard this word from my grandmother's lips while eavesdropping on a conversation between her and my uncle. My youngest *mamoo*[2] had fallen in love with an English lady and wanted to marry her. My grandmother, *Amejan,*[3] was horrified.

"I cannot have a *dou nas laa* grandchild," she stated in a firm but quiet voice.

She had me spellbound. I could not tear myself away from the conversation, even though I knew that if I was caught, I would be in trouble. The word was so musical that it had a rhythm, so much so, that I kept repeating this magical word to myself for a long time, even after the incident subsided. Little did I know that nothing good comes from eavesdropping and that the word would haunt me later in life. I did not know the meaning of the word and was excited that my future cousin would be strangely different from all of us. I repeated the word over and over again, almost like a singsong. At twelve, any word that

---

[1] (Pronounced dough nus-laa). Mixed racial children—a racially derogatory term used for Anglo-Indian children who are of mixed British Indian parentage.
[2] Mother's brother.
[3] Mother's mother.

sounded so dangerously stirring warranted investigation, so I sneaked back to the room to hear the rest of the conversation.

"We are culturally different; we don't share the same values, and most importantly, we belong to two different faiths. The child will be at a disadvantage."

This time, she said it more gently, beseeching my uncle to understand. *Mamoo*, who had just turned twenty-two, did not understand why a child of mixed race would be handicapped in a country that the British had colonized for eighty-nine years and that the child would be branded as an Anglo-Indian, a derogatory word used by native Indians of the Indian subcontinent.

It did not matter to *Amejan* which part of the Indian subcontinent her daughter or sons-in-law came from as long as they celebrated the same religious holidays, prayed together, ate *halal*[4] (Muslim kosher) food, and followed similar traditions. My four *khaloos*[5] came from faraway places in various sizes, and colors. Although they spoke different languages, they could converse with my grandmother in her native tongue, Urdu. My grandmother did not object to their inclusion in our family.

The oldest among them was my father. He was married to my mother—*Ammi,*[6] the eldest in her family of seven siblings. My father, *Abbu,*[7] was from Bengal and spoke Bengali, although he was quite proficient in Urdu.

---

[4] Kosher.
[5] Uncles married to my mother's sisters.
[6] Mother in Urdu language.
[7] Father in Urdu language.

Abbu was very tall, slim and had a golden complexion. He was an athlete and, I am told, the best sprinter of his university. On the other hand, Ammi was petite with dark-brown hair with a reddish tint and a fair complexion that would burn if she stayed out in the sun too long. She was the eldest of five girls, and my grandfather was proud of her beauty. *Amejan* never failed to tell me that while my grandfather's ancestry could be traced back to Iran, *her* grandparents came from the foothills of Mongolia. I would listen wide-eyed to the stories of my great-grandparents living in large round tents and riding bareback on their *takhi.*[8] As she spoke to me about their connection to the horses, I fell in love with these small wild animals, even though I had never seen them.

"Our spirit animal is the horse. No matter where you are, the horse will always be your spiritual guide."

"But what if there are no horses around me?" I questioned.

"They will appear in various animal forms; you must recognize them as they will give you *heshara.*"[9]

I thought of my dog, Dopey, a free spirit—untrainable, with a mind of his own. He was defiant and prone to stealing eggs from the chicken coop. Our cook called him a *'junglee'*[10] dog and said he could not be trained since Dopey would not listen to anyone except me. That was because I would bribe him with hard-boiled eggs. I decided that Dopey was my *takhi,* and when no one was

---

[8] Wild Mongolian horse.
[9] Signs.
[10] Wild.

looking, I removed his collar and let him run wild. Dopey
was an Australian ridgeback and could pass for a *takhi,* as
both horse and dog shared a ridge of fur running down
their backs.

My third *khaloo*[11] always rescued me whenever I was
caught with a boiled egg hidden in my pocket. He would
distract the cook long enough for me to slip the egg from
my pocket into his enormous hand, which he kept
purposely behind his back. I called my uncle *(khaloojan)*—
my beloved aunt's husband. *Khaloojan* was as tall as my
father, muscular, and very handsome. He had dark, wavy
hair that curled like the waves of the ocean and eyes that
were warm, turquoise. I only saw him irritated when asked
about his ancestry. *Khaloojan* prided himself on the fact
that his ancestors were Greeks who had not returned home
with Alexander, allowing them to settle in the beautiful
valley of Swat in Pakistan.

At every family reunion during Ramadan,[12]
*Khaloojan* made a point to include his famous *diples* (thee-
ples), a Greek dessert consisting of dough rolled into thin
strips, fried in hot oil, and then covered in syrup and
walnuts. Sometimes, he would prepare a small batch of
*tahini halwa* (a fudge made with tahini—sesame paste—
along with almond butter, sugar, hazelnuts, and pistachios.
That was my favorite, and he always made sure I got two
pieces on my plate before serving it to the others.

Religious holidays were very special to my *Amejan.*

---

[11] Mother's third sister's husband.
[12] The month of fasting in the Muslim calendar.

During these occasions, she would always surprise us with varieties of *halwa*—fudge—made from sesame seeds, poppy seeds, carrots, beetroots, eggs, semolina, and nuts of different varieties. My favorite was and still is, *nashaste ke halwa*. This translucent fudge is made from frequently washed semolina cooked with palm sugar and saffron, and layered with rose petals, slivered pistachios and almonds. Every bite filled my nostrils with the sweet perfume of saffron and rose. It could transport me to *Amejan's* garden, where she cultivated roses, jasmine, and gardenias. I loved to be in her garden and felt very special when she would ask me to accompany her in the evenings to make garlands from jasmine flowers. I never missed an opportunity, no matter what, for I knew I was sure to hear stories of *tikhi*, the wild horses of Mongolia.

Young as I was, I realized that it was essential to *Amejan* that family members share the same cultural values and lifestyle and observe the same religious holidays. This brings me to my youngest *khaloo*. My youngest khaloo, *Khaloo Abba,*[13] was not much taller than my aunt, although he had the lightest complexion in our family. For a long time, we thought he was a *naga,*[14] a shapeshifter, *a* half-human, and half-snake with magical powers. He had green eyes and hair so light that, at night, he looked white like a *Sheshnaga*—the white cobra favored by the gods in Hindu mythology. *Khaloo Abba* was different from the rest of us in appearance and

---

[13] Father-through aunt's husband.
[14] Cobra.

mannerisms. Although gentle and soft-spoken, his voice could turn icy cold if we spoke too loudly or failed to do as we were told. He *was Amejan's* favored son-in-law. Her face would light up with a beaming smile whenever he entered the room. She always made time for him, no matter what she was doing, and would pretend that she needed a break from all our chatter, although we knew better.

*Khaloo Abba* came from Northern India, where people spoke polished Urdu, otherwise known as the King's Urdu. We spoke *Calcatian-Urdu*, a hybrid, adulterated form of Urdu in which two other languages, Bengali and Hindi, coalesced. Throughout their conversation, most of which we could not follow even if we tried, we would sit there spellbound, listening to them, not understanding most of what was being said but hypnotized by his chant-like voice. Although *Khaloo Abba* was always kind, we were in awe of him and not gutsy enough to tell him what we thought.

I have always had a strange relationship with cobras. I didn't fear them as others did, thanks to *Mali,* my gardener, and my friend. I could identify most of the flowers that grew in the garden when I was barely six years old and name each flower based on its scent, much to *Amejan's* delight. It pleased her, and she often boasted about all my unusual talents. The credit for my so-called talent should go to *Mali,* who tutored me. Each time I misnamed a flower and got the wrong flower-scent combination, he would shake his head.

"*Choti Bibi,*[15] what do you hear after the end of the early morning call to prayer?" he asked.

He was referring to the *fajr*[16] prayers that Muslims offer to thank the Almighty for guiding them as they begin their new day.

"The singing of the birds," we chorused together.

"Yes, the birds call out to each other because they are thanking The Almighty God for the fresh fragrances that they are experiencing. Each bird's call is in praise of the Creator, as they are the first to experience this gamut of fragrances. But the sun, he is jealous. Once he is high up in the sky and has a full view of everything in the world, he gathers all the fragrances for himself, and we are left with just hints. So, *Bibi,*" he said, "if you want to experience the full scent of each flower, you will have to get up early. Your winged sisters and brothers will help you identify the flowers' names and scents."

"What if I am late?" I asked curiously because I did not like getting up so early and sneaking past my parents.

"Well then, you will get the leftovers of what the sun and clouds leave behind. Sometimes, there is nothing left," he would say with a resigned expression on his face.

I loved *Mali.* He spent so much time with me and was so clever that I did not want to disappoint him. He knew how to make plants healthy and fat by taking diluted cow-dung water and feeding the new plants with it. *Mali* showed me how to take two branches from two separate

---

[15] Little lady.
[16] Early morning prayer before the sunrise.

flower bushes, *joba*—hibiscus and *katgolap*—frangipani, join their ends by taping them together with thin muslin, and perform what he called 'a marriage.' He would place the newly married couple in their brand-new apartment made with freshly prepared soil. When new leaves sprouted, he called them '*farangee*[17]—transcontinental children—and we would spend happy hours choosing names for each new leaf. It was an exciting game, but became tedious when the leaves started growing faster than the names we could come up with. I named the new shrub *jobgolap*. *Mali* was not happy with the name. He felt the name implied that the shrub had split parentage, which it did, but did not express its new lineage. I felt that my name for the shrub was more appropriate. *Jobgolap* has a choppy sound; we chopped two branches and joined them together. The new leaves and branches from this union were of dual heritage; although the flowers had the petals of the *Jobgolap*, they were white with bright orange centers like those of the *katgolap* flowers.

Years later, after my eavesdropping incident, I referred to the *joba/katgolap* shrub as *dou nas laa*. I had a special fondness for *Jobgolap,* as it replaced my cousin since my uncle did not marry the British lady, and I never had the chance to play with my *dou nas laa* cousin.

---

[17] A Hindustani word borrowed from Farsi—*Firangee*— is similar to the Arabic word *Firanj* meaning French or Franks and rose during the medieval interaction between the Arabs and the European crusaders. In the Muslim world, the word refers to all Anglo-Europeans.

# Kalu

It was an early winter morning, a time when the scents from the garden were most intense. I woke up early and slipped into the garden to sing with the birds, whistling along to their calls and letting them know I was there. A baby cobra was hiding behind the gardenia bush. I panicked and ran to *Mali*, screaming, "*Shaap, Shaap,*[18] its hood is raised!" *Mali* just looked up from where he was and smiled.

"Oh, it's just a *naga*, the hooded king of snakes, but he is a hungry young prince. Go and get him some milk."

I ran as fast as my feet could carry me to bring a small saucer of milk for the 'prince,' which I put at a safe distance from him. *Mali* told me to be very still. I watched, spellbound, as the *naga* slowly swooshed, slithered, and moved to the bowl of milk. I was transfixed. Unlike Dopey, the *naga* did not lap up the water but moved his lower jaw to suck up the milk, just like us humans. I was utterly convinced that *Khaloo Abba* was a *Sheshnaga*[19] and that he had decided to keep his human form. I vowed to myself that I would watch *Khaloo Abba* next time he drank water to see whether the creases in his lower jaw would

---

[18] Snake.
[19] Cobra king.

suck up the water like my *naga.*

*Mali* told me that *nagas* were unique cobras, and they could change their appearance from snake to human for special females like me, and that they only came to females who could change into *naganis.*[20] I called my *naga* Kalu, which means black, because he was a black cobra and because it sounded very similar to *Khaloo.* Every morning, I brought my *naga* milk and watched him from a distance, getting bigger and longer.

One morning, while I was sitting on the red stone bench that overlooked the lotus pond, *Mali* came and stood close to me, and we both watched in silence as Kalu drank his milk.

"*Choti Bibi,* do you know the story of Raju, the *naga* who went in search of his *nagani*?"

"No, *Mali*, tell me, tell me!" I was so excited.

"Let's get closer to Kalu so he can hear this story as well. I'm sure he has heard it from his parents, which is why he is here."

"A long time ago, when four-tusked elephants rampaged the villages, and flying monkeys terrorized the cities of Prithibistan, *nagas* and *naganis* lived far away in the kingdom of Nagaistan, which could only be reached by crossing five turbulent oceans and thirteen raging seas. The seas were so vast and treacherous that humans who tried to sail on these seas never returned home. Of the few *nagas* who surfed the ocean waves of these turbulent seas to visit the land of the humans, only a few returned to

---

[20] Female *nagas.*

Nagaistan, and the few that returned kidnapped the best and most beautiful girls and turned them into *naganis*, never to return to their parents. Although it was a fairytale, young girls from Prithibistan did not venture out after dark.

"While they were aware of each other's existence through stories from their ancestors, their paths never crossed, although sightings of *nagas* surfing on the back of huge waves continued to circulate among the Prithibis.

"On the night before the young prince Raju of Nagaistan was to choose his *nagani*, he had a dream of young Princess Parul, who lived in the kingdom of Shantinagar in Prithibistan. As the sun was getting ready to retire for the day, he saw her sitting on the high rocks surrounding the city's shores, looking out at the ocean. Her long black hair flowed over her shoulders in big waves like ocean breakers, and her green eyes stared at the horizon like she was waiting for someone to appear. Her whole body glowed like the colors of the setting sun. She was calling Raju's name, and Raju saw himself on the ocean waves, swimming toward her. On waking, he knew that she was his future wife and that he would have to cross the oceans and ride the seas. Though his father, the king, objected, no matter the obstacles, Raju was determined to find a way to go and get her."

At this point, *Mali* stopped, but I could not stop myself from crying, "*Mali*, please continue the story!" I had to know.

He smiled, shook his head, and walked away.

"I'm tired; I will continue another day."

By now, I was convinced that *Mali* was right. Kalu was a *naga* prince, and I was his *nagani*. I was no longer afraid of Kalu, although I did keep a distance between us. I could not understand why *Mali* always found some excuse not to continue the story. One morning, I ran to greet Kalu with a saucer of milk, but he was not there. Kalu was gone as suddenly as he had entered my life. I felt devastated and betrayed. *Mali*, waiting for me near the lotus pond where I had brought my saucer of milk, walked toward me and sat down quietly to comfort me.

"You cannot own a *naga, Bibi*; he's a free creature and can come and go as he pleases. He will never forget you, *Bibi,* and even though you are his *nagani,* he cannot live in your world. A *naga* never forgets." *Mali's* words did not comfort me; instead, they brought out my worst persona.

"No," I cried, "Kalu is like Raju; now I know why you did not finish the story. Kalu is mine; I fed him daily so he could grow to four feet long. I brought him milk even on the coldest mornings. He was the size of my hand, *Mali*, don't you remember?" I sobbed.

"He would have died if I hadn't fed him every morning. I don't want to hear the end of the story. I know Raju didn't get his Parul. He was afraid to cross the oceans. Kalu was afraid, just like Raju!"

My petulant behavior had taken over my personality, and I couldn't heed anything *Mali* was trying hard to teach me. *Mali* sat me down on the high grassy ground close to the pond and said quietly, "You are wrong, *Choti Bibi*. One day, when you're ready, I will finish the story of Raju and

Parul."

I did not care to hear the story. I was inconsolable. *Mali* just patted my head and let me get over my loss. As years passed, I lost interest in the garden and forgot all about the *naga* I had befriended. I made fewer visits to the garden, pulled a Kalu on *Mali*, and stopped visiting him. Even now, I wince when I think of my shameful conduct. Humans and *nagas* are not so different.

Little did I know that Kalu was to teach me another lesson on human relations.

I was sixteen years old, and it was graduation day. I woke up early, glad I would wear my school uniform for the last time. My convent school days were over. I was no longer a truant prisoner of British scholastic rules. Feeling reckless, I disregarded my mother's unwritten rule and skipped making my bed.

College, here I come. No more dress codes, no more plaits. I can wear my hair exactly as I please. No more nuns pulling me aside to tie my straight, long hair so tightly that my scalp hurt or, for that matter, Mother Bonniface using a dog leash on me because I was defiant and 'a bold girl.' I felt a new sense of freedom as I skipped down the open verandah to my mother's bedroom when I heard a terrifying scream. It came from my bedroom, and I recognized the voice of my longtime nanny, Shusheelah. "*Goukra Shaap*,"[21] she screamed. I rushed to my room, and a nine-foot cobra stood on the floor on its tail with its hood raised, ready to strike Shusheelah.

---

[21] Cobra snake.

"Kalu? Is that you?" I said softly, my eyes widening in amazement. Whether it was my voice or simply the new presence, in the next second, I found myself face-to-face with the *naga*. His hood covered my entire face, and our eyes locked. I cannot remember how long I stared into those green-gold eyes because that is where my memory of the incident ends. The rest is related by Shusheelah, who had a flair for drama. Much as I try, I draw a blank, even today.

According to Shusheelah, the *naga* wrapped itself around my legs to the top of my shoulders and, in a flash, just disappeared into thin air, which we know is impossible. When I came out of my stupor, I rushed out to see where the naga had gone; it had simply disappeared. Shusheelah was in hysterics.

"He came for you; he came for you," she screamed. "Now he's gone."

She ran to the verandah, and I followed her. Naga (or was it Kalu?) was nowhere to be seen. I ran to find *Mali*, who was out in the tool shed.

"*Mali*—" I started to say, but *Mali* interrupted my sentence.

"I know. He came to see you and bid you goodbye."

"So it was Kalu?" I asked excitedly.

"If you want him to be," he said softly.

I was so excited that I failed to notice what was happening around *Mali*. When my gaze finally focused on the surroundings, I was surprised to see that *Mali's* tools were gone, replaced by unfamiliar clothing and equipment. I immediately realized they belonged to the gardener who was taking his place. Impetuous and self-absorbed, I had taken *Mali* for granted. *Mali* was leaving us.

I looked up at *Mali* and noticed for the first time that *Mali* looked different. His strong shoulders were hunched, and his gentle hands trembled as he showed the new gardener the placement of all the garden tools. I always believed that *Mali* was related to Kalu. He had the same coloring. He was as dark as ebony, with coal-black eyes that shone brightly like the large star Sirius in the night sky. His straight black hair was always tied neatly at the nape of his neck. Quick on his feet, he could be in two places at once, and his soothing voice could always calm my petulant behavior.

Looking at him now- older and wiser, with his snow-white hair still tied in a ponytail at the nape of his neck- the only familiar aspect was his kind, gentle, and soothing voice.

Tears streamed down my face as I hugged *Mali*. He immediately removed my hands from his waist. I had crossed the line, as always. But *Mali*'s nobility would remain constant.

He unclasped my hands from his waist, took my right hand, placed it on my heart, and said, "For every living thing, there is a star in the heavens. When you see a shooting star, it's the star throwing down a ladder for us to move on to our next existence. Every star has a duty. Find your star, *Bibi*."

I was sobbing so hard that I could barely form words. *Mali* continued as though I had voiced my question.

"Finding your star among the billions in the night sky

is difficult. If you are always searching, only then will you discover it. We are all born to fulfill a specific calling. You must find yours. The garden has taught you many lessons; now, little star, you will need to coexist with all the other stars and apply everything you have learned."

These were his final words to me, for although I never saw *Mali* again, his voice is always there to calm me when I am troubled.

# The Storm

*Things fall apart; the center cannot hold;*
*Mere anarchy is loosed...*
*The blood-dimmed tide is loosed, and everywhere*
*The ceremony of innocence is drowned.*
  — *The Second Coming* by W.B. Yeats

It was December 1970, and East Pakistan was in turmoil. It began with the devastating November cyclone. The Bhola cyclone was named after the devastation of the city of Bhola in the Barisal district, which included all the neighboring islands around the district. To date, it is the worst tropical cyclone recorded in the country. In that district alone, one hundred and sixty thousand plus people were killed out of the five hundred thousand people dead. The twenty-foot storm surge, created by winds as high as two hundred mph, not only devastated countless offshore islands but also annihilated entire villages, destroying crops and livestock.

The Pakistan government did not provide any form of relief. *Ammi,* a dedicated social worker, worked alongside local relief organizations to provide relief services to the affected people. I used to accompany my mother during these trips. However, the sights were so horrific that I began to have nightmares, and I was no longer allowed to go with her.

One day, I overheard her talking to *Abbu*, saying that her next trip would take her to the Bhola district and that she would be close to Andar Char, an island village formed by the continuous shifting of the river.

"Isn't that where our *mali* was from?" *Abbu* asked. *Ammi* nodded and began to change the topic, but I had heard enough and immediately insisted that I wished to accompany her.

"We must find him, *Ammi*, and bring his family to live with us. I must go with you to ask the people about his whereabouts."

"But we don't even know his name?" she replied.

"It doesn't matter; I can describe him. *Ammi*, I must go. Only I can find him."

I looked at both my parents and noticed my mother beseeching my father to stop my pleading, but *Abbu* understood differently. He had instilled in me that when the heart rules the mind, the mind must acquiesce. *Abbu* recognized that I must go, no matter how dire the situation was. I had informed Abbu about Kalu's visit and my ignoble behavior toward *Mali*. He realized that I would never forgive myself if I did not try to find him.

"You acted dishonorably in the past; perhaps this is your chance to redeem yourself. My only request is that you don't speak *Urdu*[22] during this trip—not even to your mother."

I looked up at him, perplexed. "What do you mean? I

---

[22] The official language of West Pakistan.

30

only speak in Urdu with my family. You don't allow English to be spoken with the family. That only leaves Bangla, which I use in school. I am not as fluent with it."

"That's the condition."

After a few seconds, he added, "Maybe it's time you polished your Bangla. Times are changing."

"Whatever," I said under my breath and nodded my head.

"I mean it," he said very sternly.

I had never heard *Abbu* speak to me in that tone and knew he meant business. The cyclone had wiped out the coastal plains and islands. Many of those killed outright were asleep when the storm surge struck. Thousands more died from starvation and diseases caused by floodwaters.

We were going to Andar Char three and a half months after the storm, and the chances of finding *Mali* and his family were slim. Still, I felt empowered.

Surprisingly, even the storm of the century could not deflate the spirits of the people of East Pakistan. It was the third time in twenty-plus years that an East Pakistani had won the presidential candidacy. Sheikh Mujibur Rahman, the Awami League candidate, had won and was declared the future Prime Minister by the then-martial law administrator, Yahya Khan. Mujib was well known to us.

My father and brother visited Mujib in March to deliver the relief money collected from the district of Chittagong, which included eleven towns and cities. Mujib's world-famous March 7th speech inspired young people to believe that the moment to emancipate and liberate our lives had finally arrived. My younger brother, who was eleven years old, shared the same patriotic spirit that ignited in all the youth and accompanied my father on every trip. Filled with the same optimism, I was convinced I would find *Mali*.

As we flew over the devastated shores of the broken land, my heart sank when all I could see were a few standing structures. It was as though a giant hand had cleared everything clean and left rubbles of what was. Yet it was not a clean slate, for as the helicopter descended, one could still see some of the bloated corpses of animals and what appeared to be puffed-up human bodies. I turned away from the window to switch off my overactive imagination. I would not allow anything to shake my confidence.

It was March 20, 1971 —a date etched in my heart — when ChottuBindu walked into our lives. We landed on Andar Char Island mid-morning and were all ushered into a makeshift bamboo shelter. Large water containers, packages of rice, and lentils were stacked neatly in rows of ten. Facing these rows on the other side of the shelter were tins of evaporated milk and bottles of mustard oil. *Sarees*[23] for the ladies and *longies*[24] for the men were neatly laid out on tables. A separate table was stacked with children's clothing, organized by size and gender. As the crowd

---

[23] Unstitched piece of fabric, 6 yards' long and 2 ½ feet wide that is arranged around the body like a robe with one end attached to the waist while the other rests over the shoulder like a shawl.

[24] A long wrap like kilt for men, approx 6 1/2 feet long and 2 1/2 feet wide.

surrounded us, there was much confusion due to insufficient supplies. I could only see a sea of heads among a wall of bodies, so I climbed up onto a chair and asked whether anyone had seen *Mali* or knew him. I described him to whoever was near me, as I had strict orders not to leave my spot, but I was ignored. There was nothing left for me to do but shout, "*Mali, Mali,*" hoping somehow, he would hear me. All it did was draw attention, although others at the shelter thought I was affected by all the destruction surrounding us.

Above all the din, I heard a critical voice shout, "Why are you calling *Mali*? Don't you know his name? Are you from West Pakistan?"

I was taken aback but quickly recovered to shout back, "*Mali's* my friend. He taught me gardening, and I am not from West Pakistan. What makes you say that?"

"You don't speak as we do; you sound like someone who has studied the language."

"I'm from Chittagong, so I have a Chittagonian accent," I replied.

"Oh," she said, "but you sound like a *bedeshi*."[25]

My mother must have had ESP because she dominated the conversation, explaining to the lady that my education with English nuns was the reason I did not have a local accent. She shot me a stern look and instructed me to be quiet and avoid engaging in conversation with others.

"How am I going to find *Mali*?" I wailed.

"You were told that it would be impossible to locate

---

[25] Foreigner.

him; however, your father encourages your foolish ideas, so search for Mali's face in the crowd."

Not to be outdone, I looked for the highest table, put a solid wooden chair on top of it, and climbed up on the chair seat so that I could see over the heads of the crowd. I was unsure what *Mali* looked like, for the *Mali* I remembered was not the same person I had seen last. Would I recognize him even if I saw him? While these questions were rushing through my mind, my eyes fell on a little girl, not more than four years old, standing all by herself, disengaged from the others. She was tiny even by my standards, as I was not a big girl for my age. There was something about her as she stood there, disengaged from the clamoring crowd. I was pulled to her like a magnet, and found myself looking into the palest honey-colored eyes.

"*Tomar nam ki*?" [What's your name?] I asked in *Bangla*[26] in my most gentle voice. There was no need for the question. I knew who she was. She had the same deep ebony-colored skin, and her hair, although short, was as black as the night sky. Still, I repeated my question.

"ChottuBindu, "[27] she said in a soft voice.

"Where is your father?" I whispered, my voice trembling.

"*Jaani na. Ghurni jhor amaar abba ammake ke kothai niya galo*," [Don't know, the ocean surge took my father and mother somewhere.] She said quietly.

---

[26] Language of East Pakistan, now Bangladesh.
[27] Small Drop.

I lifted her into my arms and took her to a quiet corner in the shelter, where she shared what had happened to her when the island surged. This is her story:

'Before the water hit my body and face, I remember my father carrying me across the yard toward the palm grove that grew around our house. I don't know why I woke up because the night was so still and quiet that even the crickets were silent. The only sound was my father's feet and his breathing. "Where are we going, *Baba*?" I asked him.

"We're going to heaven, but I must tie you up to the tallest *taal gatch*[28] to bring the rest of your brothers and sisters to join you. You must be very quiet as I will be tying you up very tightly; it might hurt you a bit."

I was sleepy and confused, so I said, "Yes, *Baba*, I will not cry. You can tie me as tightly as you wish."

*Baba* climbed the palm tree with me on his back till we reached the *taal phal*[29] hanging in clusters at the top. He told me to hold on to the trunk while he tied me to it. The ropes around my body and legs were so tight that I wanted to cry out, but I didn't. *Baba* told me that a storm was coming, and this was the safest spot. I would have to be strong and stay there till he came back. He slid a closed pocket knife into a little bag and tied it to my waist, tucking the bag inside my pants. I could feel the hard metal against my skin. It was so quiet. I must have fallen asleep because I woke up to a continuous roar like that of the Bengal tiger,

---

[28] Palm tree.
[29] Fruits of the Palm tree.

but ten times louder. The ground shook, and the tree bent over, but I stayed tied to the tree, waiting for Baba to untie me. I called for *Baba* many times, but my voice did not carry because I was too high and the wind was strong.

I moved my head around to see if I could draw someone's attention, but the village had disappeared. All I could see were broken-down walls, trunks of trees, and dead cows and goats. I remembered the pocket knife in my dress pocket, so I cut the rope, untied myself, and lowered myself. Since then, I have been looking for *Baba*, *Ma*, *bhaiya*,[30] and *didi*[31] for all these months. I come to every gathering to look for them. I have been hiding in these large gutters so that people don't take me away from here. *Jhour*,[32] my dog, stays with me and protects me from vultures, snakes, and people.

With my face wet with tears, I looked at *Mali*'s last gift to me.

*"Tumi kainow kaan chou, memshahib?"* [Why are you crying, *memsahib?*][33] she asked.

*"Khooshite, tomar ke peye."* [So happy I found you.] I took her hand and went to my mother. "This is ChottuBindu, *Mali*'s daughter." The three of us were locked in what seemed to be a time warp, which was finally broken by my mother, who stared at the little face in front of her and, without a word, picked up ChotuBindu and carried her to the table at the far end of the shelter.

---

[30] Brother in Bangla.
[31] Sister in Bangla.
[32] Storm in Bangla.
[33] Foreign lady in Bangla.

Humming so softly under her breath, *Ammi* removed ChottuBindu's soiled clothing. Next, her thin, fragile body was gently washed with soap and water, removing all the months of dirt and grime that had accumulated on her skin and hair. All this time, I just stared at my mother. I had never seen this side of my mother. To this day, I am not sure whether she believed ChottuBindu was *Mali*'s daughter, but the fact that I thought ChottuBindu was *Mali*'s daughter was enough for *Ammi*.

She broke the silence by saying, "Are you just going to stand there, or are you going to bring her some clothes and a pair of sandals?"

ChottuBindu's star-struck expression had carried over to me. I, too, was seeing my mother for the first time with awe-struck eyes. My mother was not as expressive as my father. She was a hands-on person, very matter-of-fact and to the point. Compassionate but not demonstrative, in control, and never impulsive. She did not wear her heart on her sleeve. I suppose she left that to my father, who had enough emotions for all of us put together. My mother was the rock; she knew when to act, and there was not an occasion that she did not meet with grace and beauty. Beautiful inside and out, she is the guiding force who has taught me to use my intellect and restrain hasty impulses, even though, at times, it is necessary. To this day, living a new life away from the country that was home, I rely on my father's wisdom and loving embrace, but I walk under my mother's umbrella.

# The Human Storm

And then came the Storm that swept every nook and corner of our land. None was exempt. The celebration of winning the elections was short-lived. The West Pakistani warlords were unwilling to concede to an East Pakistani winning the general election. On the 26th of March 1971, Mujibur Rahman, the leader of the Awami League Party, had won the election for the prime minister position and was jailed by a coup d'état, engineered by the self-appointed Military President Yahya Khan, with the full blessings of the West Pakistani leaders, including Zulfikar Ali Bhutto (who went on to become the President of Pakistan). On that same day, Operation Searchlight went into effect. I heard about it on the radio, since *Abbu* wouldn't agree to television in the house. He was convinced we would be inundated with what he called 'mind-crippling' commercials.

"But what about news?" I asked. "Telly gives us first-hand experience of relevant issues in the country?"

He looked amused. "You've never really concerned yourself with the goings-on in the country," and before I could retaliate, he added, "Plus, you get all the news you need to know on the radio."

Not to be outmaneuvered, I quipped, "But I do now." He turned toward me, gave me a stern look, and decided to ignore me. I knew immediately that I had pushed the subject to its close.

I was curious about Operation Searchlight. Who and what was the military searching for—criminals, freedom fighters, guerrilla fighters, secessionists, political activists? Unknown to my parents, I had joined a band of artists creating posters against the military presence, and engaging in protests. Operation Searchlight was a codename for a planned military operation to systematically eradicate the non-cooperation and civil disobedience movement. It was a movement ignited by Mujib's famous March 6th speech. What had started in the universities spread like wildfire to every walk of life, right down to the rural areas, and it seemed like the whole of the East wing of Pakistan was immersed in a cosmic dance that moved to the rhythm of courage, eager to free democracy and freedom from the hands of the Armed Forces. The entire populace was caught in the emotion of Mujib's stirring words, saying, "The struggle this time is the struggle for our emancipation."

On a few occasions, I joined students protesting against the regime by shouting out the freedom cry of *Joi Bangla*—victory to the Bangla people—and singing poet Nazrul Islam's famous 1928 song for which the British jailed him during the British occupation of India. Most students joined in the singing, and those who did not know the song hummed along as we marched down the narrow streets, squashed between rows of brightly painted row houses.

*Chôl Chôl Chôl*               March, March, March

*Urddhô gôgône baje madô*
*Nimne utôla dhôrôni tôl*
*Ôrun prater tôrun dôl*
*Chôlre Chôlre Chôl*
*Chôl Chôl Chôl...*

*Ushar duare hani aghat*
*Amra anibô ranga prôbhat*
*Amra tutibô timirô rat*
*Badhar bindhya chôl.*

*Nôbô nôbiner gahiya gan*
*Sôjib kôribô môhashôshman*
*Amra danibô nôtun pran*
*Bahute nôbin bôl...*

*Chôlre nôwjoaan,*
*Shonre patiya kan*
*Mrrityu torôn duyare duyare*
*Jibôner ahban*
*Bhanggre bhangg*

By a drum beat to a heavenly height
From earth beneath and soil's blight
Youth rise in the dawn's light,
Left, now, now, right!
March, March, March

Through dawn's door, a shattering blow
We will bring daybreak, scarlet in glow;
We will destroy the gloom of the night
And hindering mountain height,

The youngest of young, will sing a song;
That will raise the living from buried bones;
We are the ones, who will bring forth new life
With the might of our strength.

March young soldiers,
Listen with awakened ears;

| *agôl* | Doors that lead to death's |
| *Chôl re Chôl re Chôl.* | portal, |
| *Chôl Chôl Chôl* | A call to life extend! |
| | Break all doors tight |
| | and march, left and right! |
| | March, March, March |

I sang this song many times in singing competitions. Little did I know that this slogan would become the battle cry of the *Mukti Bahini*—Bangla freedom fighters—in the 1971 war of independence for the new country of Bangladesh. Throughout the history of Pakistan, students in East Pakistan started nearly all the protests against the government, coming up with riveting slogans. This was also true during the Language Movement in 1952. I especially liked *Tumi ke Aami ke, Bangalee, Bangalee*—who are you, who am I, Bangalee, Bangalee—and finally, the slogan that changed the political landscape of our country and got the attention of the military and death to three million Bangalis: *Tomar desh, aamar desh, Bangla desh, Bangla desh*—Your country, My country, Bangladesh, Bangladesh. We were unaware of the implications of what we were chanting. We were riding on the wave of an emotional surge empowered by the imprudence of innocence. Men, women, and children who knew the song greeted us by joining in. Others just waved and applauded us. I remembered the story of the Pied Piper of Hamlin and hoped we were not driving our procession to our demise. We were consumed with passion and naivety and intoxicated with recklessness.

But *Abbu* knew what his daughter was doing, even though I had not mentioned any of my student activities. In the early morning of 27th March, a morning etched into my brain, *Abbu* came into my room, woke me up, and asked me to get dressed and meet him in the library. Before I could open my mouth to inquire, he covered my mouth with his right hand.

"Don't question this time. Don't say anything. Just do as you are told."

I was puzzled as to why I was being sent to the library of all places in the middle of the night. When I arrived, my younger brother joined me, and we waited for *Abbu* to come and explain what was happening. My eyes wandered to the stacks of books lining the shelves. The library was my sanctuary, where I spent many hours reading and enjoying solitude.

Our house was built in stages, and the library was a recent addition. Shortly after the 1947 partition of India and Pakistan, *Abbu* and *Ammi's* family moved from Calcutta to the newly formed East Pakistan. *Abbu* had a month to find a place for *Ammi* and my older sibling, so he constructed a modest house with two bedrooms, a kitchen, and a bathroom. However, pregnancy affected both my mother and our home. As our family grew over the years, the house expanded as well. My mother and the house seemed to give birth simultaneously.

The house transformed into an octopus with eight arms, separated by fenced gardens. Each of these green spaces was either an orchard or a rose garden, all under the supervision of *Mali*. Each arm functioned as a bedroom-sitting room, complete with an en-suite. The living room, where we flourished as a family, was at the center, with a dining area that accommodated both large and small gatherings. The formal dining and drawing rooms, along with two guest rooms, were located on the ground floor, adjacent to the kitchen and utility rooms. We called this eight-armed structure, *Octome*. We always dined at the formal dining table, for although we typically ate with our fingers, following Muslim etiquette, each place setting was meticulously arranged with all the necessary cutlery for European cuisine. A finger bowl was always present, accompanied by hand-embroidered napkins designed and crafted by my mother. An unspoken rule at the table was that fingers had to be washed in the finger bowl before using the napkins. Yet now, banished to the library, my brother and I were far from the rest of the house and the dining room where we shared all our meals. I couldn't understand why *Abbu* had sent me to the most secluded part of our home, as the library was windowless, and its back wall faced a rundown disputed land.

Waiting in anticipation in the library, we jumped up at the knock on the door, eager to hear what had brought about the decision to move us to the library. We were surprised to see *Abbu* with a breakfast tray. It must have shown on our faces because *Abbu* set the tray on the study table, came over, hugged us, and gently guided us back to the couch, where we were both waiting expectantly for someone to arrive and explain what was happening outside our door. *Abbu's* words would change all our lives in

Octome, but more drastically for my younger brother.

"Please sit down and listen carefully without interruptions," he said in a very gentle but firm voice. He faced us both, and I noticed for the first time how tired he looked. He took my face in his two hands, and his eyes gently washed my face tenderly.

"I know about your involvement in the student processions and the painting of banners against the military regime. I'm not here to debate your bravado or foolishness. However, actions have consequences, and, in this situation, danger to life, not only yours but your family's. Concerning your brother, I am responsible. I took him on trips to deliver Cyclone Relief funds to Sheikh Mujib, who had won the election and was sure to be Pakistan's next Prime Minister. Of course, that did not happen. Instead, Mujib has been arrested and imprisoned and will probably face the same fate as Mr. Shaheed Suharwardy."

He cradled my face in his large hands, and I felt them trembling. So, in youthful bravado, I placed my hands over his to soothe them and lift his spirits.

"Don't worry, *Abbu*, I can handle it." He released his hands from my face and gripped mine tightly, so much so that my hands hurt.

"You took on something without paying any heed to its consequences. You always act on emotion and impulse, which isn't bad, but when that action, no matter how good, affects others, it becomes ineffective, if not downright dangerous." I must have appeared perturbed because the following few words would forever change my idyllic life.

"Pay attention to what I am saying next. Last night, the Pakistan Army surrounded Dhaka University. They attacked the residence halls, especially targeting Jagannath Hall and the female dormitories, killing a large number of students and taking the female students to their army barracks. Professor Jyotirmoy Guhathakura and the notable philosopher Govinda Chandra Dev, the former and the current Provost, were murdered in their homes. They also went to the homes of other professors and arrested them, although some escaped. I am told that about two hundred students were shot dead, and a warrant is out for more. I have also been informed that Bangla physicians and journalists have been abducted from their homes, and the word is out that the army is out to arrest professors, artists, intellectuals, businessmen, and engineers. I am giving you strict orders that you and your brother stay indoors, away from the windows, and under no circumstances should your voices carry outside this room."

My head reeled with all this information. "Any questions or comments?" he asked.

I shook my head. For once, I had nothing to say. The implications of *Abbu's* words finally resonated with me, making me realize that my brother and I were under indefinite parental house arrest.

# My Private Storm

My imagination soared with hidden tanks and guerrilla fighters popping out of haystacks. I pictured these metal beasts with their long snouts piercing through windows and doors, eyeing their victims, deciding whether to toast them or just blow them up. I thought about when my dog Ringo trapped a poor mouse in a corner, toying with it until he smashed the unfortunate creature with his large paws. It was a sport for Ringo, and now it is the same for the Pakistan Army. My imagination just went haywire. I could hear the firing of guns in the distance and machine guns singing their death songs, and I shuddered each time the sounds got closer, only to be relieved when they grew faint. I began to hear them all the time. I could not separate reality from my imagination. I had never paid attention to my family teasing me about having an overactive imagination, but now I was beginning to scare myself, which frightened me even more. I thought of my professors and friends and began to replace the bodies of the dead students and professors with my friends and teachers. The thought rang in my head: When would they come for us?

I could not shake off the impending cloud of doom that squeezed my insides like a boa constrictor. With every squeeze, I felt things just got worse. It all started with the brutal massacre of Bengali students, professors, engineers, and intellectuals by Pakistani military and paramilitary forces, whose informants were the *Razakars*. These volunteers, most of whom were Urdu-speaking migrants, settled in East Pakistan from Bihar, Calcutta, and Orissa; others were anti-Bangladesh and pro-Pakistan Bengalis. The *Razakars* were collaborators of the military, paid spies, and under military protection. They would point out, and partake in the killing, looting, and raping of the Bangla-speaking population who opposed not only the military takeover but also the banning of the *Awami League*—Peoples' Party—the most prominent political organization in the country. Since the language of Muslim India was Urdu, many Bengalis were trilingual, speaking English, Urdu, and their mother tongue, Bangla. My mother's family was Urdu-speaking Bengalis from Kolkata, India, whereas my father came from the landed gentry of Bengal. Like other Muslim gentry, he was trilingual, like my mother.

The crimes committed by the Pakistani army and the Razakars prompted a counter-reaction from groups of Bangla-speaking locals against innocent Urdu-speaking East Pakistanis and Urdu-speaking Bengalis, including us. Thus, my father and mother became targets, depending on who was wielding the guns. A significant divide existed between the local Urdu-speaking and Bangla-speaking families and us, and what exacerbated the situation was our British education, which positioned us in an upper-class category within the population.

Although my younger brothers and I were born in a

sovereign land free from the chains of colonization, Pakistan in 1956 was still tied to the British Empire as a member country of the British Commonwealth. Our parents were still pretty much under British sorcery that turned newborn Indians and Pakistanis, like my father and mother, into native English men and English women. And we, the children of post-colonial parents, were so far removed from our own Bangla culture that we genuinely fit the term *duo nas laa*. My grandmother had indeed made the right call regarding my uncle's desire to marry the English lady, but she had based it on race. I, on the other hand, saw *dou nas laas* as individuals of cultural *khichree*—a potpourri of different languages, habits, customs, and tastes, swimming in cultural seas, unaware of how far we have drifted away from our origins or what kind of cultural current we are drowning in.

While these thoughts were racing through my mind, I immediately focused on what was happening in Octome. The safety of the families of my *ammi's* sister, *Khala*, and her husband, my *Khaloo*, plus *Ammi's* youngest brother, *Mamoo*, and his family, became necessary, and preparations were made to accommodate them. On the 29th of March 1971, my second *Khala* and *Khaloo, Mamoo, Momani—Mamoo's* wife—and their son, my baby cousin, joined us. We were also joined by our Christian cook and his family and by our Hindu nanny and her family, all fearing the onslaught of the guns. I marveled at Octome; she could expand with each addition, gathering all of us in her arms, holding us close, much like a mother hen roosting her chicks. We felt safe and comforted.

Here, we thrived in the comfort of each other with a false sense of security. My K*haloo—Khala's* husband, with his great humor, kept our spirits up even when Octome was caught in a crossfire. It was a general rule that as soon as we heard guns firing, we had to hit the floor and stay there because, depending on where the shots were being fired, bullets were sure to go through some part of Octome's seventy-two windows. Most of the time, the bullets would go through one window, clear the room, and out the window facing the parallel wall. The only safe place was the floor, as the crossfire could last for minutes, for what seemed like an eternity. At the first sound, we would hit the floor on cue. At times like this, *Khaloo* would break the silence. "Okay, everyone, swimming competition! Whoever swims the fastest on their stomach and gets to the other room, behind a solid wall, gets the first choice from the dining table." This meant that we would have to swim on our bellies, with outstretched arms forming the letter T, continuously bringing our arms to our sides while simultaneously pushing with our toes. This action would jump-spring us forward and move us from one room to another, to a place with no windows.

It was pretty comical because my *khaloo* would reach there first and describe each of our swimming movements behind the safety of a solid wall. It was not because he was faster, although taller than most of us, but because he had already planned his destination. We, on the other hand, would flounder around trying to push ourselves with our toes, lift our heads, wiggle on our stomachs, push the floor with our hands, and keep wiggling till we reached our destinations, most of the time by banging our heads on the wall. The one who got to the other side first would be grinning from ear to ear and laughing out loud until the whole room filled with laughter. Of course, the younger ones moved faster, getting from one room to another, while *Ammi* and *Khala* stayed last. My father and *Khalo* would have to pull their respective wives to safety and have us all rolling with laughter. It was a comedy of fear. Ironically, we looked forward to these dangerous moments as licenses to release the laughter that lay bottled within us.

I compared our lives to Anna Frank's diary. The story of a young Jewish girl whose family were in hiding from the German Gestapos in Nazi Germany. In my case, my family and I were in hiding from the Pakistani Army. Anna had to share her and her family's hideout with another Jewish family, whereas I got to stay in Octome, sleep in my bed, and be with my entire family, my uncles and aunts, not to mention all our help and ChottuBindu. I felt blessed.

The month of March, which brought joy to the land and its people, was ending. March, the month of *Boshonto*—Spring—lasted until mid-April, during which the land expressed its joy. The *Shimuli,* also known as the Red Cotton flowering tree, along with *Bokul* trees, blazed across the countryside. The Bokul tree's eight-petaled, double-tipped white flowers grow in clusters, filling the countryside and cities with a sweet fragrance. My friends and I would search for a grove of *Bokul* trees and lie beneath the shade of their large, glossy leaves, taking deep breaths and filling our lungs with their delightful scent. Among the most sought-after trees was the Red Silk Cotton tree for its *Shimuli* flowers. This leafless tree, adorned with a gorgeous crown of fleshy orange and red-orange flowers, measuring six to eight inches across, was a stunning sight. The five-petaled flowers form cups filled with nectar, delighting birds and bees. My friends and I would carefully sneak under the *Shimuli* tree—a difficult task due to its thorny trunk—to watch the *doyel*, or oriental magpie-robin, sip the syrup from these beautiful, nectar-filled blooms. Their songs would attract other robins, and soon, all that could be seen was orange, red, and black against the blue sky. I suppose it was nature's way of heralding the arrival of the new month of the new calendar year—*Boishak*—Summer.

Summer, the first season and the first month of the Bangla calendar, blazed the sky with the Krishnachura blossoms, my favorite flowering tree. The orange-red, five-petaled flowers made the trees look like giant powder puffs of red. I defied my father by sneaking to one of the remote windows so as not to be denied this exhibition. This was the time of the year when marriages were performed throughout the country. Brides in the subcontinent of India and Pakistan wear outfits in red, red-orange, and gold, ranging from *saris* and *lehengas* with blouses to *gharara* and *shalwar kameez* with *dupattas*, all heavily embroidered with gold and silver thread. I was convinced it was the land calling for new life by its blazing voice, reminding us that reunion brings joy. I was convinced. So, I threw caution to the wind, left the library, went to my parents' bedroom, sat on the floor close to the window where I could have a full view outside, and flooded my eyes with the blazing vision of the Khrishnashuras.

*Boshonto* is the last season of the Bangla year. The Bangla calendar is comprised of six seasons. Each season consists of two months, totaling twelve months. The six seasons begin with *Summer* (*Grishmo Kal*) from mid-April to mid-June; *Monsoon* (*Borsha*), from mid-June to mid-August; *Autumn* (*Shorot Kal*), from mid-August to mid-October; *Dry* (*Hemonto*), from mid-October to mid-December; *Winter* (*Sheet*), mid-December to mid-February, and the last season of the year, <u>Spring</u> (*Boshonto*), from mid-February to mid-April. To create even more confusion, those of us who attended missionary schools, studied in English, and followed the Gregorian calendar found the twelve months of the Bangla calendar to be a challenge.

The first season of the Bangla year, *Grishmo Kal*—Summer—is celebrated nationwide with great enthusiasm and joy. It falls in the month of *Boishak.* The New Year, or *Pohela Boishak,* is the third most celebrated day in the country. Unlike the other two days of celebration, which are the Muslim religious holidays of *Eid ul-Fitr* and *Eid ul-Adha, Pohela Boishak* is a public celebration that involves all religious groups. It occurs on the fifteenth of April in the Bengali month of *Boishak.* The Bangla calendar consists of twelve months, starting in April and ending in March. The new Bangla calendar begins in summer and ends in spring. Since my convent schooling had only familiarized me with the Gregorian calendar, I struggled to understand the Bangla calendar; it just didn't make sense. I found it challenging to comprehend the Bangla months, each of which began in the middle of a Gregorian month.

## Bangla Calendar

Boishak (April 15–May 15), *Joishto* (May 16–June 15), *Ashadh* (June–July), *Shrabon* (July–August), *Bhadro* (August–September), *Aashwin* (September–October), *Kartik* (October–November) *Ogrohayon* (November–December), *Poush* (December–January), *Magh* (January-February), and *Faalgoon* (February–March), *Choitro* (March–April 14).

While we, post-colonial children, followed the Gregorian calendar inherited by the country, which incidentally included all missionary-run schools and metropolitan and governmental life, the rest of the country adhered to the Bangla calendar. To keep us further estranged from our heritage, January 1st was designated as a government holiday. Unlike the rest of the populace, we celebrated it enthusiastically in private clubs and five-star restaurants, which eagerly awaited the month of *Boishak* to celebrate the New Year.

While all these thoughts swirled in my head, I sneaked into my parents' bedroom and made myself comfortable on the floor. Next, I peeked out of the windows that lined the wall, through which I could feast my eyes on the rows of Bokuls, Shimuli, and Krishnachura trees in the distance. March had ended, and we found ourselves in the middle of the Bangla month of *Choitro*, the last month of the Bangla calendar. March prepared us for the upcoming New Year celebration of *Poila Boishak*. My mind drifted to the various types of *petha*—rice cakes—from petits fours to large *Chunga Pitha*—rice cakes stuffed with coconut palm, sugar, and thickened milk—that were sold on the streets. I envisioned the flowers and fruits that intoxicated my senses and delighted my taste buds. I inhaled deeply and recalled the scents of the different mangoes the family enjoyed. The aroma of countless varieties and flavors of mangoes is ingrained in the DNA of every Bengali; once captured by the allure of mangoes, we Bengalis are their captives forever. Although the land is home to two hundred and seventy varieties of mangoes, I was only familiar with ten, of which *Langra* was *Abbu's* and my favorite. But that was not all; *Grishmo Kal* (summer) brought us lychees, jackfruits, and pineapples as sweet as honey; *sharifa* (custard apples), *chikoo* (sapota), and guavas with sweet rose interiors, blackberries that stained lips a deep red, and crispy white berries that added a delectable crunch to salads. Next came leeches, star apples, and *chalta* (dillenia indica).

I recalled when my mother took me to the fruit and flower bazaar. Rows of fruits and flowers were deliberately arranged on opposite sides of the brick walkway, allowing the aroma of ripe fruits to blend with the scents of gardenia and jasmine, creating a heady mixture that intoxicated my senses and left me savoring a rhapsody of pleasures. This unforgettable sensory experience is triggered whenever I encounter gardenia and jasmine garlands or visit fruit bazaars. In either case, I am transported back to the bustling backstreet bazaars. So, even though *Bosonto* is the last season in the Bangali calendar, it remains the season we all eagerly anticipate.

As I indulged, lulled by my memories and with my eyes basking in the fiery plumage of the Krishnachura trees, I noticed, with the coming of twilight, the redness in the distance growing brighter and shifting to a yellow-orange hue. It seemed the Krishnachura flowers were getting more intense as I reminisced. I gazed lazily at the scene when I suddenly sensed something was not quite right. A burst of flames shot up into the air, confirming the obvious. The row of houses that bordered the trees and separated them from us was on fire, and the flames were moving toward Octome.

Throwing caution to the wind, I stood up and ran past all the open windows, screaming, *"Ghar me aaang lag jaigi. Khirki ke bahair dekhiye."* [The house will catch on fire. Look outside the windows.]

*Abbu* looked at the flames I was pointing to, which were racing toward Octome, and called the fire department without hesitation. I can never forget my father's phone conversation with the fire department. It is etched into my memory bank and will remain locked in my nightmare box forever.

"There is a fire outside our home; it rages from the Circuit House's east side toward Asghar Dighi, and our house is directly in its path. Please send the fire department immediately."

I will never forget the look on his face as he carefully placed the phone down on its cradle, turned around, and looked me straight in the eye.

"The fire service is now under military control, and our area is not a priority. I spoke to him in Bangla, as it's a local fire station, which turned out to be a mistake."

*Mamoo's* wife, a Punjabi from West Pakistan, yelled, "What do you mean they are not coming? Are they just going to let us burn?"

My youngest *momani* was loud, fierce, and spirited. She ran, picked up my little cousin in her arms, much to his surprise, since she never had much time for him. She then grabbed the phone, asked my father for the telephone number, and dialed it, all in a matter of seconds. She let out a torrent of Punjabi, the language the army man spoke. This was not unusual because the Pakistan Army, primarily Punjabis from West Pakistan, was sent to terrorize and subjugate the East Pakistanis.

Once calm, my aunt returned to her usual boisterous, loud self, laughing and carrying on with him, pointing to the window, describing the fire, and painting a picture of our fears. The little bit of Punjabi I could understand was about the fire and the number of people in the house. While she was chatting with the military gentleman on the phone, *Abbu* had me collect all our passports, transcripts, and schoolbooks, secure them in a carry-on, and pack some clothes, shoes, and essentials for my brothers. As I rushed to collect these necessities, I could hear my aunt's high-pitched voice crying, laughing, joking, and asserting that we were all Urdu-speaking Pakistanis, and that the only Bengalis were our house help, which was not true. I thought my aunt had gone quite mad.

My Punjabi aunt, like the rest of the family, was also trilingual, but instead of Bangla, she spoke Punjabi, the language of Punjab. Punjab, the largest province in West Pakistan, also supplied the Pakistan Army with the largest number of soldiers. In East Pakistan, Bangla was a common language spoken by all, even though different dialects were spoken in other districts. West Pakistan, which consisted of four provinces, had its respective major languages of Punjabi, Sindhi, Pashto, Balochi, and Saraiki. Urdu, a migrant language, was made the official language of Pakistan, although English has been the de facto language since 1947.

I recalled a conversation with *Abbu* about the government's unreasonable decision to impose the Urdu language on all Pakistani nationals. Why did I speak Urdu at home and attend an English-medium school where I studied Bengali as a second language? I was at school with kids facing similar circumstances, separate from the typical school-going children. I had sought an explanation.

This memory transported me to a different time warp, and I found myself in our garden, pruning rosebushes with *Abbu*. It was one of those cherished moments.

The rose garden was *Abbu's* handiwork and his pride and joy. Nestled between the two wings of Octome, this two-thousand-square-foot garden was designed by *Abbu*. The rose garden was connected to my parents' bedroom by five steps leading to a covered semi-circular verandah. A large glass door, nine feet by nine feet, connected the verandah to the bedroom. The garden was enclosed by twelve-foot walls, punctuated only by a small doorway linking it to the rest of the gardens of Octome.

Each time *Abbu* traveled to West Pakistan, which was quite frequent, he returned with a single rose cutting. *Mali* always looked forward to his return to Octome. These roses were rare in East Pakistan, and *Mali* was thrilled that his garden was the main topic amongst the *malis* and other gardeners. Mali boasted about his garden's exotic collection of roses, calling each rose by its unique name. I loved listening to him pronounce some of the English names of the rose bushes, even though sometimes it was difficult for him to form the words. But that did not deter him. If I tried to help him articulate it correctly, he ignored me and continued calling the shrubs by his pronunciation. I believe, to this day, that he was taking ownership of the shrub by using his version of the name.

*Mali* tended to each rose bush with a level of care that would put any mother to shame. When all the *malis* got together, they compared notes to see who had the best garden. *Mali* always won. He would intentionally call out names such as *Soufaid Rani Gulab* (White Queen Rose), *Dil ki Roshani* (Light of the Heart), *Damascus ki Shehzade* (Princess of Damascus), Midnight Queen, and Zaituna, a beautifully shaped rose moschata originally from Iran. This rose was *Mali*'s favorite; he referred to it as *Shoupnor Mala*—the garland of dreams. With its rich, honey-gold color, this rose was truly stunning. In the moonlight, the velvet texture of its petals glistened like Manuka honey.

*Mali* spent considerable time tending to these foreign additions, much to Sadu's displeasure. When *Ammi* pointed out Sadu's culinary shortcomings, particularly the absence of herbs in his cooking, Sadu retaliated by blaming *Mali* for neglecting the herb garden. The true reason *Mali* enjoyed caring for the rose bushes was that it allowed him to be near *Abbu*. *Abbu* would engage him in conversation, recounting all the beautiful rose gardens he had visited in Rawalpindi and Lahore, especially the Shalimar Gardens in Lahore. *Mali* was an attentive listener, and *Abbu* took pleasure in sharing the history of all the rose cuttings he had brought back from West Pakistan.

*Abbu* took pleasure in his rose bushes, and I cherished our time together, discussing anything that popped into my mind. This time, the topic was the Urdu language. I sensed he felt uneasy talking about it, but I urged him to explain. His expression turned somber, and I instantly regretted my words, but it was too late. He pulled me in close and then, looking away, began to speak more to himself than to me.

"I cannot begin to understand why Jinnah decided to establish a language for the country that's not spoken by more than three-quarters of the population," he said, half-aloud, more to himself than to me. "Perhaps he thought that a new country with a common language would foster a new generation of Pakistanis united by a shared tongue. In Jinnah's wildest dreams, he could not have anticipated the 1952 Language Movement in East Pakistan. You must remember, *beti,* that with the birth of Pakistan in 1947, President Jinnah, an Urdu-speaking migrant himself, chose Urdu as the official language because it was already the *lingua franca* for Muslims in the north and northwest of British India. Urdu also served as the literary medium for colonial Muslim and Hindu writers from the Northern Provinces, Bengal, Orissa, and Bihar, extending down to South India. Remember, my child, the official language of the Mughals, who ruled India for almost three hundred years, was Farsi and Urdu," *Abbu* explained. "Your grandfather, my father, spoke five languages and wrote in four—Farsi, Arabic, English, Urdu, and Bengali."

"Yes, *Abbu*, but he was a subject of the British Raj," I quipped impertinently.

"You forget that we were conquered and colonized for almost a hundred years. I was born a subject of the Raj," he said gently but firmly, ignoring my cheekiness.

"But not I, although we are their *dou nas laas*. We are exactly what Macaulay wanted us to be," I retorted.

*Abbu* was surprised that I knew about Lord Macaulay's speech to the British Parliament.

"How did you know about that?" he asked with surprise, though I detected a hint of pride in his voice.

"I took civics as one of my courses, and when Professor Nani Gopal heard us speaking in English to one another, he directed us to read Macaulay's July 10, 1833, speech to the British Parliament regarding Indian education and the strategy that would keep us forever bound to their heritage."

"And what did you learn?" This time, I could hear the pride in his voice.

"Can I quote, *Abbu*?"

"Of course, *Beti.*"[34]

---

[34] Daughter.

"And I quote, *Abbu*: *'We must at present do our best to form a class who may be interpreters between us and the millions whom we govern; a class of persons, Indian in blood and color, but English in taste, in opinions, in morals, and in intellect.'*"[35]

"He was talking about remolding us, *Abbu*; he was talking about forming *dou nas laa*s."

I must have mouthed those words aloud because I was pulled out of my time warp and found myself back in the room with my brother, shaking my shoulders. My mind felt scrambled, leaving me restless, anxious, and fearful. I wanted to finish my flashback memory and explore the *dou nas laa* notion that had haunted me throughout my youth, but instead, I grabbed my brother's hand, and he looked at me in confusion.

"Are you daydreaming again?" He said. "We don't have time for you to go into one of your weird moods."

"I must have dozed off," I replied quietly. Exploring the *dou nas laa* theory would have to wait for another time.

My brother was seven years younger than I, and we were always very close. We were instructed to stay inside so that the military would not find us during the evacuation. We remained in the library while the rest of the house got ready for evacuation, waiting for a family member to come for us. We waited.

Time passed, but nobody came. I held my brother's hand in silence, our eyes fixed on the clock opposite us. It

---

[35] Macaulay's '*Minutes on Education*,' Feb 2, 1835, is published in Henry Sharp's *Selections from the Educational Records of Education, India 1*. (Calcutta, 1920), cited hereafter as 'Sharp').

felt as though we were in a time warp, and the library was a time capsule. Even the clock in front of us had stopped. To our relief, the door opened, and *Ammi* walked in.

"We didn't have to evacuate. The fire is controlled and will not affect us, so everything is okay."

Relieved, we both ran and hugged *Ammi* tightly. The Fire had subsided, and the army-controlled fire brigade had left the grounds. Although Octome had withstood the blaze bravely, the flames scorched the back wall that faced the raging fire. *Ammi* told us to join the rest of the family for dinner. It was a joyous moment. We were all happy to be together once more.

That evening was a quiet one. We basked in each other's company. My brothers took turns playing chess with my *khalu* and *mamoo*, and my *khala*, *momani*, and I chatted and reminisced. *Abbu* and *Ammi* just sat quietly, comfortable in each other's togetherness, occasionally joining the conversation, happy to have us all together in the safe arms of Octome.

# April Fool Day

Early the next morning, my youngest brother came charging into the library.

"Guess what? The Pakistan Army is leaving, and the *Mukti Bahini*[36] has defeated them. Now, we can all go back to the way things were."

A surge of relief filled my entire body, lifting me from the bed. I was giddy with joy, all dangers forgotten. I hugged my brother and raced toward the front door to witness the army retreating. But before I could make ten feet from the bed, I heard my brother shout behind me, "April Fool!"

I froze, standing dead on my feet. I felt like a deflated balloon—round and robust, full of energy, soaring high toward the heavens, only to be punctured by an annoyed bird on flight whose territory the poor balloon had invaded. Squashed and spent, I went back to my bed and sat down. Baffled, my brother ran up and put his arms around me, confused by my demeanor.

"I'm sorry, *Apa*. I thought you would realize it wasn't true because today is the first of April."

---

[36] Bengali freedom fighters turned forces that included soldiers from the East Pakistan armed forces, paramilitary, and guerrilla resistance citizens.

"Of course, it's April first. I was pretending to be fooled so you would believe my whole expression. I know it's impossible to defeat the Pakistan Army."

But I was fooled. It was April 1st, the 18th day of the Bangla month of *Choitro,* the eleventh month of the Bangla calendar. It was also the 5th day of *Safar,* the second month of the Islamic calendar.

I wondered why we engaged in this ridiculous custom. We were not British, and it made no sense to designate the first of the month as a fool's day. Why was it in April? I thought. This day fell in the middle of the Bangla month of *Choitro.* Spring was ending, and we were entering the summer season. The air, sweetened by the fragrances of fully blossomed Sheuli and Bokul flowers, put everyone who came in contact with it in a heady mood. Spring brings new life, and summer nurtures it to fruition, so why play a joke on others during a month when nature begins to renew life?

In school, we were taught to greet each other in April with the phrase, 'April showers bring May flowers,' while also trying to play tricks on our friends during the same month. All these inconsistencies exhausted my already weary brain, which now felt convoluted.

"Let's go find *Ammi* and *Abbu,*" I said quietly.

Drained by all these thoughts, I needed my parents' comfort. I put my arms around my brother's shoulders, and together, we walked out of the artificially illuminated library into the natural light.

Days crawled by uneventfully, so much so that Abbu decided we could return to our bedrooms. I was happy to return to my room, and to my surprise, I found that the room had been picked up, the bed had been made, and everything was in place. I rushed to the window, flinging it wide open to let the morning sunshine flood the room. I could hear the Koeliya's *khuhoo khuhoo* calls, affirming that no matter what destruction humans caused, nature was still there to sustain life and beauty.

I don't know how long I stood there, basking in the sun and taking deep breaths of the menagerie of scents that abounded outside. I basked in nature's bounty; life was good. I had my entire family—uncles, aunts, and all who worked for us. I was thankful. I stuck my head out the window, opened my mouth, and took big gulps of the sweet, fragrant air that permeated outside. April, the last month of the Bangla calendar, is connected with the spring of the Gregorian calendar; in both cases, nature showered the land with flowering trees and intoxicating scents.

New beginnings, fresh scents. New life starts in spring, no matter how we structure our calendar or label the months.

It was heartwarming to be with my parents, uncles, and aunts once more. Occasionally, I would join Sadu in the kitchen to see what new concoctions he had fashioned from the army's meager rations allocated to each household. Sadu amazed us with his ability to turn rice and potatoes into delicious cakes, pancakes, and dumplings; and lentils into meat -like delicacies.

Days went by, and before we knew it, nine days had passed. We were getting accustomed to our new routine of staying within the walls of Octome. We played pretend games, taking turns acting like we were visiting friends, going on a picnic to Rangamati, or speedboating on Kaptai Lake.

I looked forward to the evenings when we took turns sharing our make-believe adventures, even though maintaining these brave facades was challenging. Each day blurred into the next, and with each passing day, I began to withdraw emotionally from everyone around me. I sensed a change within myself that I could not quite grasp. I would snap at my brothers, and even when *Ammi* asked me to do something, I would pretend not to hear her or act sulky. I was a brat; if anyone noticed, no one called me out. It felt as if I had been given full permission to be difficult.

But *Abbu* did notice. It was the morning of the ninth of April, and like the day before, I walked around, consumed with myself, not paying attention to anyone in the room. I felt a hand on my shoulder, and as I was about to shrug it off, I heard *Abbu's* voice. It was not his usual voice; instead, it was razor-sharp, cutting into my present state of mind.

"I am disappointed to see you become someone I don't recognize. Where has my daughter disappeared? You act as though you don't have all your family members with you who love you. We have much to be grateful for, *Alhumdulillah*—praise be to Allah. You have your father and mother, your brothers, your *khala*, *khalu*, *mamoo*, *momani*, and little cousin, yet you wander around as though everything has been taken from you. Allah does not love thanklessness or ingratitude."

The power of *Abbu's* words punctured the dam of tears built up inside of me. I was sobbing so hard that *Abbu* had to hold me in a tight embrace, allowing the raging river that was blocked up inside me to burst forth. As I hugged *Abbu* and nestled in his arms, I could not stop my ceaseless crying; and like the river, I heaved and spilled my tears all over *Abbu's* shirt.

"You are like a raging river. Now I need to change my shirt. It is soaking wet," *Abbu* joked, lightening the mood and giving me a moment to pull myself together. One of *Abbu's* rare qualities was his ability to heal an open, bleeding wound and stitch it up seamlessly, leaving no trace for anyone to see or discuss. He let me pour out all the angst gnawing at my insides, and now that I was spent, the matter was settled. There was no need for an explanation. *Abbu* is a father made in Heaven.

"It's good to feel and feel intensely, but sometimes that can become a weakness. Everything in moderation; that's what Islam teaches us. This does not mean you should not care, but when that caring takes over your good sense, you may act out of compromised emotions."

I felt a quietness within. The intensity of my feelings slackened, and a calming determination flowed through my previously angry veins. I was ready to ride each day to the full.

The sound of machine guns firing somewhere in the distance was a given; we were all getting used to it. Occasionally, we would hear an isolated rifle shot coming from the killing fields of the Chittagong Circuit House, where the Pakistan Army had established its military base.

When that happened, we would stop our activities and say a small prayer, hoping it wasn't someone we knew. I was aware that the army would abduct people from their homes and take them to the Circuit House to be executed and discarded in a mass grave somewhere on the grounds. Although I pretended not to hear the gunfire from the Circuit House killing fields, my ears always managed to catch my father talking on the phone and praying for the person whose name was mentioned. Curiosity would nudge me to ask who the person was, but common sense always prevailed, and I held back.

I once heard him say to *Ammi*, "He is with Allah now, in a better place. *Inna lillahe wa inna ilayhi rajeoun*—from Allah, we have come, and to Allah, we will return. That no one can change." *Abbu's* voice was tired yet strong. *Ammi* held him close, and they remained quiet in each other's arms. In that moment, I prayed that I would strive to nurture *Abbu's* unwavering belief in the strength of his Islam—his submission to Allah's will. Nothing happens outside the will and knowledge of Allah. A passage from the Quran came to mind: the 8th verse from the sixty-seventh chapter of the Quran:

*"Do they not see the birds above them with wings outspread and (sometimes) folded in? None holds them [aloft] except the Most Merciful. Indeed, Allah is the All-Seeing of everything."* Al-Quran, 65:19.

"If everything is under Allah's control, then why does Allah let bad things happen?"

*Abbu* smiled. "It is a question many ask," he said. "The Quran clearly states we are 'the caretakers of the world, and a position we desired and accepted.' Allah offered it to other created beings, such as the mountains, but they all refused to take it. We boldly embraced a significant commitment, becoming the vicegerents of this world and everything in it. Yet, Allah also says in the Quran: 'Allah is The One Who created Death and Life to test which of you is best in deeds. He is Allah the Almighty, All-Forgiving." 67: 2.

"The Quran reinstates that our actions create reactions; this is the principle of cause and effect. When bad things happen, it is our actions that cause the harm. Therefore, we must address the wrongs we have committed. We are accountable for our actions because each of us is granted the free will to distinguish right from wrong. Never forget this, *Beti*."

"What if we choose to do wrong? Isn't what the army and the Razakars are doing wrong?" I asked.

"Then we must stop, rectify, and compensate for the wrong done, ask Allah SWT for forgiveness with sincerity, and never indulge in it again. Allah SWT is Compassionate and Merciful, and we must pray to be forgiven."

"I will apologize to all, especially to Sadu and ChottuBindu. I believe I have been ugly to them."

"Yes, to them. There is no need to apologize to the family; they understand."

They did, and days passed slowly. Each day felt both long and short. The same routine dragged on. I couldn't get used to the regularity of events and wished something exciting would happen to break the monotony. Each day felt like a week, and I stopped checking the calendar, reminding myself that only a single day had passed since the next morning. I felt guilty for not being grateful for our good fortune. I rebelled against feeling guilty, then turned around and rebelled against my rebellion. I felt emotionally twisted, searching and hoping for anything that would pull me out of my destructive state of mind, not realizing that my wish would soon be granted.

# The Un-Wish

Chittagong. April 10<sup>th</sup>, 1971. It was unusual in the early days of the month of *Boishak* to be pelted with torrential rains. I remembered *Mali* telling me that rain in *Boishak* was nectar for the parched soil of *Boshonto* that followed. April was a dry month and could be unbearably hot. When I would complain, *Mali* reminded me that the hot weather was needed for ripening the mangoes, pineapples, and lychees—the fruits I loved to eat. Now, too, the rain pounding hard against the windowpanes was a blessing, as it drowned out the sounds of gunshots and, at the same time, nurtured an unnatural tranquility in Octome. We were all actors playing our roles, moving like sleepwalkers, twirling within our centers, attuned to our compasses.

Lulled by this soothing environment, I retreated to my bedroom, pretending to work on my writing, occasionally interrupted by my younger brother, with whom I had grown quite close. We had spent uncertain days together in the library, which helped forge our bond.

Most of the time, I spent alone in my room. I had pulled my writing desk close to the window so my eyes could wander outside my bedroom and visit the gardens of Octome. Today, however, my gaze freed itself from the confines of Octome to fly over to the charred *Krisnchura* trees in the distance. I felt a shiver run down my spine. There was something in the air—a disquieting silence—that I brushed aside, reminding myself that civil war is brutal. *Abbu* had shared that part of our history with us.

Visions of the 1947 partition of India flashed before me, made vivid by the constant gunfire echoing in the distance, the charred trees, the distant cries of people, and the terrified screams of children whose parents were being taken away by the military.

This time, I found myself amidst the chaos caused by the 1947 civil war and the partition of India into India and East and West Pakistan. The British had lost their prized possession, India, and were eager to leave the country in turmoil after they haphazardly divided it into two sovereign nations—India and Pakistan—based on their views of Hindu and Muslim-populated regions. Was that possibly out of revenge? I wondered. Surely, they realized that Pakistan split into two parts with India in between, could not survive for long.

What was Jinnah (the Pakistani advocate for partitioning India) thinking? Why did he accept the presidency of this two-part, newly formed country, Pakistan? What was Nehru, the advocate for the Hindu majority, up to? That crafty old fox—Jinnah—was no match for him. The only person who could compete with Nehru in strategy, wits, and cunning was Shaheed Suharwardy, who opposed the division of India into religious sectors and the separation of Bengal.

The primary purpose of the division was to provide the Muslims and Hindus with their own homelands, separate from one another, so they could coexist peacefully. How could Pakistan ever be complete when the country was never a single entity to begin with? It would be like Mexico owning Texas and New Mexico as they once did, and anyone from Louisiana wanting to visit family in Phoenix, Arizona, would have to travel all the way up to Colorado before heading down to Arizona. It just didn't make sense to me.

Was Jinnah just plain stupid, or was he so hungry to be president of a new country that he had not worked out the details of what it meant for a country to be bisected into two parts separated by a hostile country? Was it revenge that made the British dissect Bengal and Punjab arbitrarily? The Radcliffe Boundary Commission, which took its name from Sir Cyril Radcliffe, could not draw a clear line separating the Muslims, Hindus, and Sikhs either in Punjab or in Bengal. So, it was an arbitrary division.

I felt my body shake, only to realize my brother was shaking me. Since my younger brother and I were confined in the library, he assumed he had earned the right to enter my room unannounced. No amount of reprimanding dissuaded him, so I just locked the door when I did not wish to be disturbed.

"What's going on, and why are you sleeping near the window with the sun beating down on you? Aren't you hot?" he asked.

"I must have just dozed off. It's none of your business, and what are you doing in my room?" I felt a bit ticked off.

He caught me at a critical moment, trying to make sense of Jinnah's decision, which created the present situation in our country's short political history. Plus, his air of being my equal because of our history together in the library was beginning to irritate me.

"You didn't knock again or ask for permission to come in. If you do it again, I will have to report that you're disrespecting my privacy."

"I'm sorry, *Apa*. Can I stay now? I don't want to be alone. I feel something strange in my stomach that I can't explain. I don't want to throw up; it's just something happening inside that I can't communicate to anyone. Everyone seems so busy with what they're doing."

"What is wrong? What do you feel?" I asked, speaking in a less irritated tone.

"I don't know. I feel something heavy inside and around me, which scares me." He paused and continued, "I sense a great weight hovering over Octome, ready to fall and crush us at any moment."

I could see that he was sincere in his feelings. My brother and I had inherited what Abbu jokingly referred to as a sixth sense. While I had better control over mine and could push it away, he was still too young to manage it effectively.

"Octome is too big and built like a tank. I don't believe anything can bring her down. I think you are just imagining this whole thing."

But he was right. I had felt it, too, and could not figure out what it could be. We were all together, safe, and withstood the fire. Yet I, too, had experienced something similar earlier this morning but had decided to bury it. Now, his fears opened channels I did not wish to explore.

"You know what," I said with a forced, unnatural laugh, "let me tell you about what happened in 1947 during the partition of India when *Abbu* had to take *Bhaiya* to the hospital amidst the fighting mob in the streets of Calcutta."

"I know that story, and you weren't even born yet." He was sure I was attempting to distract him from what he was feeling.

"It's not a story. Do you want to hear about it?" He gave a disinterested shrug at that point, although I could see I had captured his attention.

"Okay, you were told that *Bhaiya's* tonsils were infected and that without surgery, he wouldn't survive, right? You weren't informed about the circumstances *Abbu* had to go through to reach the hospital. Am I correct? But you weren't given the full account *of* Abbu's encounter with the mob. So, let me tell you the whole story."

"Now, close your eyes and listen to the gunfire; envision the blazing flames behind Octome and immerse yourself in the streets of 1947 Calcutta. Park Circus Maidan, the field where all the festivities occurred and where *Abbu* and *Ammi's* flat stood, has transformed into a battleground between Muslims, Sikhs, and Hindus. Houses on both sides of the broad street are either ablaze or being invaded and looted. There is chaos, pillaging, and violence all around. Can you visualize that in your mind's eye?"

"Amidst all this, imagine *Abbu* running through the streets, dodging gunfire and men wielding daggers and ropes to hang anyone who seems like a threat. Anarchy and mayhem reign supreme. Children are torn from their parents, witnessing their fathers being struck down and their mothers being assaulted. *Abbu* is running; you know he can run fast. As a student, he was the fastest sprinter at the university where he now teaches. But the mob is closing in on him as he passes Lady Braburne College, where *Ammi* was finishing her master's degree before marriage. Picture this: *Abbu* is caught by the Hindu mob, and…"

"What do you mean? *Abbu* would never let the Hindu mob catch him; he was a first-class sprinter." My brother looked at me reproachfully, upset that I had tarnished my father's athletic abilities.

"It's true. Hear me out."

I pretended to be annoyed but was glad he was engaged in my story. The ugly part of me just wanted to let him stew in his anxieties a bit longer, so I shamefully pretended to be upset for a few minutes and continued with the sequence of events.

"Picture this: *Abbu* is caught by the mob of rioting Hindus. A young man draws his knife, misses *Abbu's* head by inches, and cuts him in between the eyes, and…"

"That's not true. *Abbu* got that as a child when he fell down the stairs."

"*Shush*! Don't be so loud. I am getting tired of your interruptions! Do you want to hear what happened to him with the mob? I can stop, and we can sit quietly."

He shook his head. The little 'fish' was hooked. "Please, no interruptions this time."

"Okay, so as *Abbu* stands there bleeding, blood

streaming down his face, he lifts *bhaiya* onto his shoulders to free his arms and speaks in polished Bangla,

"*'Tomader ki hoyache? Ak joun Firengi, akta line tene amader Desh ke bhange diache ar Amara bandorrayer motoun nach techi, loot techi, nijer desher bhai boune ke je maarte chi. Amar baap dada, tomar baap dada ak shonge ai desher mati te jonmo hoaichi, boro hoiyeche. Akhon kaar rokto mati te porte che? Amra ki shiklum? Bish bido loi (university) theke ki bodhi Neelum? Akhon Firengira desh ke bhange diyeche, ar ki baki? Amader rokto, Amader dhonsho. Tikache, amar rokto chao amaar cheler rokto chao? Ni ye now Subhan Allah, La ila ha ilAllah.'* [What has happened to all of you? A no-good Firengi—a derogatory term for the British—has drawn an arbitrary line rupturing our beloved Bengal, and we, like their pet monkeys, are singing to their tunes, looting and killing our fathers, mothers, brothers, and sisters. Our fathers and grandfathers grew up together, eating the dirt of this land. This land is our flesh, our bones; its waters run through our veins, and we breathe each other's air. It is our blood that is being spilled, not the Firengis! They came here under the pretext of trading. They saw a land blessed by God; they saw riches beyond their imaginations, and they killed and took what was not theirs. And now, like silent robbers, they are leaving. But what have you learned all these years under their captivity? Is this what Gandhiji, Shaheed Suharwardy, and we Bangalees wanted? This is the land of Rabindranath Tagore and Nazrul Islam, of Hindus and Muslims. What is the use of going to universities for higher education if your mind can be so easily controlled? My son and I are ready if it is my blood that you want and my two-year-old son's, then *Subhan Allah, La illaha illallah.* Glory be to God. There is no God but the One God."

Amid all this turmoil, a voice cried out.

*"Sir, apni?"* [Is it you, Sir?] *Abbu* turned toward the voice. It was a young Hindu student from his history class.

*"Topash naki?"* [Is it Topash?]

*"Hain sir, Aame. Maaf kore dain amaderke. Cholen taratri haspatale niye jajcchi."* [Yes, sir, it is I. Forgive us. Please let us take you quickly to the hospital.]

"Park Circus, where they lived in Calcutta, was predominantly a Muslim area. Muslims and Hindus had coexisted peacefully until the arbitrary division of Bengal by the British into West and East. Overnight, this region became India. Confusion, anger, and bewilderment manifested similar to raging *Haatis* (elephants) trapped in the *Khedda (corrals)* of these newly formed borders. Muslims found themselves in West Bengal, and Hindus in East Bengal, both charging against the man-made barriers that Radcliffe had constructed to confine the people of Bengal. It was as if *Kali* had been unleashed upon this defiant land that had long resisted the British, and now *Kali's* thirst could only be quenched by the blood of her people."

I was struggling to continue my story, so I felt relieved when we heard the door open. Instead of *Abbu*, it was *Ammi*.

"Where's *Abbu*?" Her face told me nothing.

As I stared at her, my eyes searched the space behind

her in hopes of finding my father's beautiful face, but I could not break through the thickness. My heart beat so fast that I thought it would stop.

I felt my mother's arms around my shaking body.

"They took him. There's nothing we can do but pray to *Allah SWT*." (Allah the Most Glorified, The Most High). *Inshaa Allah* (If God wills), he will return.

A sound came out of my body like a giant tidal wave that swept my body and dissolved my world into a lump of dust that slowly dissolved into nothing. I turned to look for my brother, who stood frozen. The next instant, my mother's arms were around us. She held us close until our bodies relaxed. This was the second time I remember *Ammi* displaying her emotions to us. *Ammi* is the resilient bamboo that grows outside the walls of Octome, and like the bamboo, cyclones can bend her but not break her. At that moment, I promised that I would mold myself to be just like *Ammi*.

# Shadows

Chittagong. April 11th, 1971. The last few days of the month of Choirtro were ending, and the arrival of Boishak—the first month of the Bangla calendar—was near. The sun shines high in the sky, yet there is no light; a sea of gray envelops Octome and everyone living within her. I am surrounded by grayness without the white or black light to guide me.

It has been four hours since the military took *Abbu*. The day is stretched like a tense piece of elastic, ready to snap. Nothing stirs, and we move around like sleepwalkers. I cannot remember when this day started, and have no idea how it will end. All I know is that today, *Abbu* was taken by the military. Today is also my brother's birthday—a day of celebration.

*Abbu* always celebrated our birthdays by telling us stories of our early childhood, some of which he fabricated. He would make it interactive so we could play along for fun. There was always a lot of history, arguing, questioning, teasing, and just laughing at the absurdity of it all. *Ammi* would join us with our favorite dessert: mango tapioca pudding laced with saffron and rose water, tubs of mango ice cream, and *aam murabba*—crystallized, stewed raw mangoes—on the side. We took a spoonful of this heavenly concoction, rolled our eyes, smacked our lips, and sang praises of her culinary skills. *Ammi* would smile and pretend it was nothing so worthy of praise, but we knew, looking at her face, that she was pleased.

It was not just the game we looked forward to, although *Abbu* was a convincing storyteller, but also the unique desserts made exclusively for birthdays. Some of the stories *Abbu* would tell us were so absurd that we would try to stare him down, not believing a word of it. But he would look at us with a straight face and ask how we could refute it since we were too young to remember. The game was trying to catch *Abbu* repeating the same story on different occasions so that we could call him out.

This time, it was different. *Ammi* came in with our dessert and looked at us with a fake surprise expression since none of us made a move for the dessert.

"Have all the storytellers in my household gone to another country, or have they all been captured by the enemy?"

We stared at her in disbelief.

"What do you want us to do?"

"So, who's next in line to uphold the tradition? This dessert is for storytellers and their audience."

She looked at me and said, "Did you not witness your brothers coming into the world? Surely you must know the circumstances at that time."

I sat quietly, not wanting to participate. I could not read *Ammi's* expression. She was acting like nothing disastrous had happened. I could not—would not—allow my fears to cross over to my brothers, although every time I heard gunshots from the direction of the Circuit House, where the executions were taking place, my heart just stopped, if only for a second.

I immediately made a silent prayer for *Abbu*. I remembered the verse in the Quran that *Abbu* used to quote: *"Nor can a soul die except by Allah's leave. The term being fixed by writing."* (Quran, Chapter 3, V.145) I repeated this over and over to cement my trust and acceptance. I also remembered him quoting Shakespeare, *'Cowards die many times before their deaths; the brave never taste death but once'*—or something like that. He always quoted Shakespeare; to him, Shakespeare embodied expressions for contemporary society.

I realized for the first time that *Ammi's* stoic behavior was a reflection of *Abbu's* teachings. After all, she was just eighteen when they married. They complemented each other like a pen expresses itself through ink.

Theirs was an arranged marriage. The only time *Abbu* saw *Ammi* was when she was walking with her friend, who happened to be *Abbu's* niece. *Abbu* was lovestruck because, in the next few days, a marriage proposal was sent to my grandparents for *Ammi's* hand in marriage. *Abbu* was a young college professor with a modest income, despite coming from a distinguished family. *Ammi* was the eldest daughter of my *nana—Ammi's* father, who was the chief magistrate of Kolkata, India, and the apple of his eye.

I was told *Amejan* objected to the proposal because of *Abbu's* low income and age; he was only twenty-three years old. *Nana*, who took an instant liking to *Abbu,* remarked that with *Abbu's* looks and noble bearing, he would go far in life and accepted the proposal, provided *Ammi* agreed. *Ammi* and *Nana* had a special relationship, so when *Nana* told her that he had selected someone who would make her a good husband should she *choose* to have him, *Ammi* asked to see him, which she did from behind the curtain. She must have felt something for she agreed. The first time she met *Abbu* face-to-face was on her wedding night. I was told it was a full moon that night, and they spent it on the roof of his flat, talking about their dreams and all they had in common. Some marriages are made in heaven.

*Abbu* is the bravest person I know. Earlier that year, he had taken the cyclone relief money that was collected by the community in our city of Chittagong to Sheikh Mujib (the father of Bangladesh), who had been put under house arrest many times by the military. *Abbu* was unafraid of the army and had remained protected. But I reminded myself that this time, it was different. The military had taken him to be executed. So, what *Allah Subhanhu wa Ta'Allah*—The most Glorified, The Highest—has decreed, will be done. I told myself all this. It was somewhat comforting.

I wished to be comforted, and I turned to prayers, asking for what was best for my father. I prayed: "Ya Allah, *Subhanahu wa Ta'Allah*, do what is best for my father." These were long prayers, humbling myself to Allah's will. "Your will be done on earth and in Heaven. And God loves those who are firm and steadfast." (3:146)

So, I turned to my middle brother to do what Ammi asked.

"Did you know that *bhaiya* and I weren't exactly thrilled about you coming into our lives because we would be responsible for caring for you? Bhaiya thought you'd be a bother since you would want to tag along with his friends?"

"Why would you have to take care of me? I can take of myself," was his impertinent reply as always.

"Unfortunately, as your older sister and brother, we would be responsible for you, and you were quite a nuisance back then and still are. So stop interrupting if you want to know why we accepted you into the family."

My youngest brother, always the peacemaker, had the knack of cutting through arguments.

"Go on, *Apa*—older sister—tell us."

"Okay. There was a tremendous storm the evening *Ammi* went into early labor. The electricity throughout the town was out, trees were down, the main roads were blocked, and there was no communication with the outside world. Of course, that's when you, my brother, decided that you wanted to be out of *Ammi's* tummy and be a pain, as you always are," I said with a twinkle in my eyes.

This time, he did not challenge or contradict me.

"Okay, okay, what happened? Was I born then?"

I smiled and made myself comfortable, pretending to ignore him but watching him through the corners of my eyes, ensuring he was totally under my control.

"Well, she couldn't be taken to the hospital, and the doctor couldn't come to the house, so *Amejan* had to deliver you."

"No way, she is not a doctor."

*Amejan* had assisted in delivering babies as a midwife under the doctor's supervision. This time, she had to deliver her eldest daughter's five-month-old premature baby during a storm without the help of the obstetrician.

"You know *Amejan*—there's nothing she cannot do. Bhaiya and I were worried about you. First, we didn't want you to come and be a pain in the neck for us, and now you had decided to come with no doctor around, putting *Ammi's* life in danger."

"But I didn't know, *Apa*, that there was a storm. I was in her tummy. I would never put *Ammi's* life in danger."

"Anyway, we were shooed out, hoping you would stay where you were. *Bouaa*—Nanny—was busy boiling water, and *Abbu* was asked to leave the room."

"Why?" both of them chimed in together

"You know why—because *Abbu* panics when anything happens to any of us. But especially where *Ammi* is concerned, he goes crazy!"

"Then it's a good thing that the military took him and not *Ammi*," chimed my youngest brother, who had remained quiet all this time. He was my mother's favorite son, even though she denied it.

My youngest brother is a beautiful, beautiful boy. He has the eyes of a raven, the darkest of all of us, with eyelashes so long they curl over, accentuating his eyes. Like a raven, his coal-black hair glistens in the sun, creating a striking contrast against his pale gold skin. He is nine years younger than I am, and I feel responsible for him. I squeezed his hand to comfort him, for he is not as vocal or boisterous as his older brother. I continued.

"Bhaiya and I had fallen asleep. When we woke up, we ran to *Ammi's* bedroom. *Amejan* met us at the door and asked us to wait. She returned with something tiny in her arms, wrapped in soft cotton. And there you were—a premature, nine-inch-long, pinched-face baby. In your tiny, tiny hands were these enormous, beautifully wrapped bonbons. 'Look what your brother brought you from heaven,' Amejan said, smiling at our cautious faces. We still didn't trust this little mite who would become the center of attention, hold our parents' time and affection, and be a nuisance to us. But then, who brings bonbons from heaven? *Amejan* was able to melt away all the jealousy and resentment we felt toward you, and we gathered around her to see your squished-up face."

"But you knew he didn't bring those bonbons from heaven, right, *Apa*? You both couldn't be that naive." Always the pragmatic one, my youngest brother wanted to ensure that we knew *Amejan* was playing the role of a therapist.

"We knew we had no choice but to accept him; he would be our flea. *Amejan's* yarn only made it easier." I said with a smile.

Before my brother could reply, we all heard the sound of a military truck stopping near our front door and then a gentle knock on the door.

Nobody moved. We stood frozen as if the room had suddenly dropped to zero degrees Celsius.

At the second knock, Momani, being closest to the door, walked over and opened it with a firm grip, bracing for the worst.

*Abbu* walked in.

Screams of joy rang in the room. Octome glowed from inside. It was as though she had transformed into an eight-petal lotus that opened itself to welcome the morning sun. Octome was welcoming her son. We danced around *Abbu*, bombarding him with questions. We all talked at once, and he tried to answer in monosyllables. Amid all this joy, my father sought *Ammi*, who had not joined us. She was a short distance away, and she was trembling.

"You should take a shower," was all she could say.

*Abbu* took one large step and pulled her to him so that she would stop trembling. My aunt gathered all of us to prepare a celebration for his return, but it was to give my parents time with each other. We thanked the Almighty for the mercy shown to us and celebrated with *Ammi's* mango tapioca saffron and rosewater pudding.

What happened to *Abbu* at the Circuit House was truly an intervention from God Almighty. We urged him to share what took place there, for it was a miracle that he returned alive from the killing fields of the Circuit House.

I slipped my hand into *Abbu's*. "Why did God save you, *Abbu*?" I asked quietly.

"I can't tell you why God saved me, *Beti*. It simply wasn't my time. But I can tell you who was chosen to be the instrument of my deliverance. As I sat in the detention room, waiting for them to take me to the field where high-ranking Bangla military suspects were executed, I prayed. At that moment, your uncle, ex-Brigadier General Badr, walked past me, stopped dead in his tracks, and turned and turned around, shocked to find me there. His expression changed when he noticed the handcuffs. He shouted for the officer, who arrived promptly. The discussions that followed were all in Punjabi, which I couldn't understand, and the next thing I knew was that Baig himself removed my handcuffs."

"'Do you know who he is!' he exclaimed in a loud voice that echoed through the room. Badr then informed the officer that I had received the highest award given to an individual in Pakistan—the Sitara-i-Quaid-i-Azam, presented by the former president, Ayub Khan. The officer apologized, explaining that he was following orders. Before I knew it, Badr guided me to his vehicle and dropped me off."

The nightmare was over. The sun had set, and the celebrations had ended; all was well. Night came, and I was restless. I tossed and turned in bed, squeezing my eyes shut in the hope of falling into a deep sleep by blocking out all traces of light. But I felt a heaviness I could not explain. The night felt off. I lay on the bed, struggling to make sense of the dark shapes entwined in my fantasies. My imagination was playing tricks, and I could not control the images. I decided to check on my brothers to break away from the looming visions that seemed to grip me by the throat, choking me until I was breathless. Seeking relief, I hurried to my brothers' room and found them sleeping soundly. As I turned to leave, I noticed the lights in my parents' room were on. So, I walked over to see if everything was okay.

This was the second time I was eavesdropping on a conversation not meant for my ears. I remembered that nothing good came from overhearing conversations. Yet I could not help myself. I overheard *Abbu* tell *Ammi* that as soon as it could be arranged, my siblings and I had to leave Chittagong, East Pakistan—now Bangladesh—immediately for Karachi, West Pakistan—now Pakistan—because our lives were in danger. In my mind, a bomb exploded, and I sank to the ground.

*Abbu* must have heard me collapse, for I woke up to *Ammi* putting a wet compress on my forehead.

"What are you doing up?" *Ammi* asked, her voice a mix of scolding and tenderness. "Hasn't it been a long day, and shouldn't you be asleep?"

I started sobbing hysterically. Tears ran down my face like a raging river dammed up for years. At first, I cried hysterically, and then, just like the river that had finally broken through its barricades, I wept quietly but consistently until my sobs became as regular as my breathing. *Ammi* and *Abbu* put their arm around me without speaking.

*Abbu* had guessed that I must have overheard parts of his conversation with *Ammi* and appeared relieved when I cried out, "Why are you sending us away?"

"Wrong choice of words," *Abbu* said, correcting my choice of words and misguided perceptions. "We are protecting your brothers and you from the watchful eyes of the military. You see, they will keep destroying us endlessly. All three of you must leave for Karachi under the watchful protection of your *mamoo* and your *momani*, who is Punjabi, where you will stay with your *khala* and *khalu* until we get there and decide the next step in your exciting life ahead," he said with a forced smile. In that brief moment, I noticed the sadness in his eyes.

"Consider this an unexpected turn of events that will guide you toward new beginnings. Do you remember Pip from *Great Expectations*?"[37]

"Going to Miss Havisham's didn't do Pip any good, and just look at how it affected his future." I retorted, angry that *Abbu* was trivializing such a life-changing decision, one that determined my identity as a *dou nas laa*. I looked at him with a quixotic expression.

"Can we talk about this in the morning?" I asked.

"Of course, *Beti*."

Deep down, I knew my fate had been decided, and I had no say in it. The foreboding thoughts from earlier that evening had manifested with a vengeance. I had always cared for my brothers and listened to their needs, but this was different. I was now solely responsible for them, whereas *Ammi* and *Abbu had made the decisions before*. This new responsibility frightened me.

---

[37] Dickens, Charles. *Great Expectations.*

# Exodus

Chittagong (Chattogram), April 12th, 1971. It's Monday, the 28th of Choitro, the 15th day of Safar, five days before we leave Octome and everything we love and know. The countdown has begun. I stayed in bed as long as I could. For once, I did not have the urge to rise and run to the garden, look out of the window to greet the rising sun, or say hello to the birds or whistle back at their calls. I was angry, scared, and confused all at once; I could not shake a gnawing fear that had grabbed me and paralyzed me in my bed. When *Ammi* came in to check on me, I closed my eyes and pretended to be asleep. I heard her sigh, and I knew she was aware that I was faking, so she quietly left the room. I felt guilty for causing her pain, but again, I thought it was unfair for her to make me feel this way. I finally decided to get up and join the rest of the family.

*Abbu* was already sitting at the breakfast table, and when I approached, he made light of my breakdown from last night.

"You should start waking up early now that you're the boss lady," he teased, attempting to lighten the mood.

I held my tongue, to his surprise. I was not going to make things easy for him. I wanted him to break the news to my brother and help him deal with the shock and dismay. Besides, anything I would say would be short of rudeness. My brothers, puzzled as they were uninformed of *Abbu's* decision, looked up with questioning eyes.

"Your sister is your new guardian. All three of you will accompany your *momani* and *mamoo* to Karachi, and we will join you there as soon as we can. You three will be traveling by ship, which departs in five days. I am sending two cars with you—one for your *mamoo* and the other for you three to get to school there. You will stay with your *khala*, who has been in your life for as long as you can remember. I have rented her flat upstairs so you can take as many things as possible while traveling by sea. You will not be alone in Karachi, as your entire mother's family is there."

My brothers looked stunned and immediately turned toward me with puzzled eyes as if to ask, *When did all this happen, and where were we?* I avoided eye contact and just looked down at my empty plate. No one spoke. My brothers looked to me to challenge *Abbu* and were puzzled when I did not speak. Their eyes accused me of betrayal, but I could not rise to the occasion and confront my father. I felt the pain in his voice and understood how difficult it was for him to make this decision. Although he was smiling, trying to lighten the situation, his smile did not reach his eyes. I did feel a bit of remorse. All this time, I had been thinking only about myself. I was so consumed by my feelings of being uprooted from my beloved home and all that I was leaving behind that I had not considered the impact *Abbu's* decision would have on him and *Ammi*. So, I decided to soothe the situation a bit.

"Yes, exactly. We have always flown over the Indian

Ocean, and this is our one chance to sail across its powerful waters," I said with sarcasm and a forced smile.

"It will be so much fun since we have never traveled by sea. We can do whatever we want because *Mamoo* and *Momani* do not follow any rules. No schoolwork, just playing games and watching the ocean for sea creatures; maybe we'll even spot some sharks! What about those so-called sea monsters that roam the Indian Ocean?"

I was referring to the elusive coelacanth, a fish with steel-blue, armored scales and fins that resemble arms, which was once thought to be extinct but has been found swimming in the waters of the Indian Ocean. Coelacanth existed from 409 to 66 million years ago and was considered the missing link between land and sea. These limb-like, finned fish are closely related to tetrapods, which include birds, amphibians, mammals, and snakes. I knew this information would pique the interest of my youngest brother, a budding scientist. "The Indian Ocean is full of these, right?"

My brothers stared at me, surprised by my compliance, which turned into excitement.

"Are we actually going by ship? When?"

*Ammi* looked away as *Abbu* ignored the sarcasm in my voice, making me regret my flippancy. I couldn't understand this urge to hurt *Abbu* when he was already suffering. Why was I trying to make him feel worse than he already was? Yet, I could not shake off the impulse to hurt those I loved. I was in pain and wanted *Abbu* to hurt too, and seeing him in pain gave me a twisted satisfaction. I felt ugly inside. I was indulging in something so selfish that it shocked me into shame, and I promised myself I would never deliberately hurt my parents again. I would do my best to support their difficult decisions, no matter how I felt.

The thought of being alone without our parents terrified me immensely, especially since we were headed to Karachi, which now felt like enemy territory. While we spoke Urdu, we didn't speak it like the people from West Pakistan. West Pakistan consists of four provinces, each with its own language. Though Urdu is Pakistan's national language, only ten percent of the population speaks it. Karachi is located in Sindh, where the majority of people speak Sindhi; those who speak Urdu do not typically have a Bengali accent. For once, I thought, my *double-edged* post-colonial education and lifestyle might be helpful, so I decided that all three of us would speak English publicly. After all, English is the official language of the government, and we were still under the constraints of post-colonial culture as members of the British Commonwealth of Nations.

Once I was able to overcome my disbelief, anxiety, and resentment, I was able to empathize with my parents' emotional duress. We had traveled all over the world together, and this was the first time we would travel without them. A wave of overwhelming sympathy and tenderness swept over me for my parents. Their decision to be parted from us was less frightening than the impending danger of our being captured by the military. I looked at *Abbu* and nodded, assuring him I understood.

Later that day, I watched *Ammi* pack our clothing and necessities for the long journey. I did not help her. My surly side made me stand and watch as she put our favorite objects in shipping trunks. I justified not helping by reminding myself that she could finish the packing herself since she and Abbu knew what was best for us. It was only when she asked her youngest brother, my mamoo, to help crate the piano that I broke down. The finality of the decision hit me. I ran to my room and locked the door. I was not going to let anyone see me cry. And no one did. I had cried myself to sleep and woke up to nightfall. To my surprise, I was left undisturbed to process my feelings and felt much better when I woke up. It was yet another lesson I learned from my mother: when one cannot change a situation, go with it and make the best of it. Lesson learned.

That night, we all stayed up late with *Ammi* and *Abbu*, soaking in their presence, memorizing my father's infectious laughter, the way they laughed together, and my mother's beautiful smile that always reached her eyes. That was when we knew she was happy. I remember her saying, "Being together as a family is a great gift life can offer. Make the most of it so you have no regrets later on." I vowed to remember that. I memorized how my parents touched each other and us, my father's elegant and ever-so-shapely fingers. This time, when my father pulled me to him and rubbed his cheek against mine, I did not pull away even though the bristles of his beard scratched my face; I memorized the feeling. My brothers jumped on *Ammi's* side of the bed, tossing her pillows around, much to her feigned protests. It was as though this moment and time had collaborated to cheat tomorrow. In that moment, we felt that our lives would remain unchanged, and the impending journey that awaited us would never happen.

# Denial

Chittagong (Chattogram), April 13th, 1971. Tuesday, five days left before we sail. I decided that, like Pip of *Great Expectations,* who resigned himself to life with Miss Havisham, I, too, would resign myself to life in Karachi. So, I decided to play my part to the fullest. I bounced out of bed to check what *Ammi* had packed, telling myself the whole time that this trip was an extended holiday, so I removed all winter attire that she had packed. It was April, and I was sure we would all return here by winter. I was going to make the most of this 'holiday' and re-engage with all my relatives from my mother's side, who left for West Pakistan at the beginning of the Pakistan military invasion. Absorbed in this thought, I did not hear the knock on the door and looked up, surprised to see that it was *Ammi* standing quietly by my side. Her eyes glanced over to what I was doing, and, without speaking, she began folding my clothes and putting them back in the metal trunk. I immediately pulled it out of her hands.

"*Ammi*, I'm not going to need any warm clothing. It's very hot in Karachi, and we should be back here by winter."

"Just take some in case you don't. Your stay could be extended."

"But that's not what *Abbu* said! He said that you both

would join us shortly and that we would come back together, right?"

She gave me a smile that did not reach her eyes and said gently, "We don't know when we might be all coming back, so it's best to take some of your warm clothing."

"What will happen to Octome, Sadu, ChottuBindu, and everyone else? Who is going to take care of the flowers and the garden?" I wailed.

"I will not pretend to tell you I know, for I don't. Your father will think of something. Trust him."

Her face was so tired that I could not continue questioning her anymore. I took the sweaters from her hand and returned them to the trunk. At that moment, the gravity of the situation hit home. I wanted to ask her so many questions, some of which I already knew in my heart. I wanted her to deny what I knew would occur in our lives. I wanted her to confirm that things would not change and that we would all live together as a family. Pictures of our lives together were moving at a heightened, accelerated speed as though the movie reel had gone amok. I wanted to stop the button and bask in the moment, but I could not. Instead, I decided to take in *Ammi's* physical presence with all my senses: her fragrance, that of day-old gardenia; her voice, which always reminded me of the *doyel* (Asian cuckoo), soft at first but which could get loud and demanding; and her gentle hands as she oiled and braided my very long, hip-length hair. Deep down, I knew it would probably be the last lone time I would have with her, and I wanted to bask in it.

Together, we sorted out the books that I wanted to

take with me. I could not recall the last time I had been in the company of my oldest aunt and her family. Would we fit in or feel like outsiders? If so, I would have much solitary time. Books were always my companions.

"You might consider taking some lesson plans for your piano practice. You have numerous music sheets that you find hard to read, often relying on playing by ear and memory. Perhaps this would be a good opportunity to catch up, improve your sight-reading, and practice all the scales."

"*Ammi*, I don't understand why we're taking the piano. Saltwater air isn't good for it, and before we know it, we'll be on our way back, and the poor piano will have to ride the ship again."

I was doing it again. I didn't want to know what she was trying to convey, and I wasn't interested in taking everything I loved to a place I didn't know. Furthermore, taking all my favorite items meant my stay would be extended indefinitely. I had no intention of staying there one day longer than necessary.

"What are you trying to say? That we're not coming back here and should take everything precious to us?" I did have a flair for the dramatic.

"You should know that your safety is our top priority, and it's simply not safe for the three of you to be here. We will follow as soon as possible, after taking care of everyone who depends on us for their livelihood. We want you to feel comfortable where you are, surrounded by familiar things. You can always bring it back. So, it's best to take it with you to play the piano and occupy some of your time. Playing the piano lifts your spirits, so you need to practice. By the time we join you three, you might be playing some Chopin."

*Ammi* smiled. She knew I loved Chopin's *Nocturnes* and that I had her attention. "Let us look at all the lesson sheets together and decide on the ones you want to take."

As I picked up the selected sheets and put them in her hands, a wave of calm spread through my body, washing away all the fears, doubts, and ugliness that had taken control of my behavior. I remembered the saying of Prophet Mohammed (peace and blessings upon him): "Heaven lies beneath the feet of your mother." *Yes*, I thought to myself, *and when your mother smiles at you with so much love, you are touched by the wings of heaven. I am going to be okay.*

# Fortitude

Chittagong (Chattogram), April 14th, 1971. I woke to the sound of birds singing. The bulbul, my lovely nightingale that serenades me every morning, reminds me to rise and join the other birds. To my surprise, Bulbul was perched in the guava tree. He flew over and settled on the windowsill. When I approached the window, he did not move away. Our eyes locked, and he held my gaze. I heard him say, *"This is not my last song; I will find you wherever you are."* He had vanished as I wiped the tears from my eyes and looked up to thank him. I glanced around, but he was nowhere to be seen. Surely, I had not imagined him, for I heard him as clear as day. Yet, the guava tree was devoid of any birds. *Ammi* had warned me about my imagination getting the better of me, and I thought to myself, *This must be it.*

Peering from the window, I watched dawn creeping up slowly behind the Krishnachura trees, accentuating their charred, blackened bodies. I had slept through the morning *Adhan* (call to prayer), so I hurried downstairs and sneaked into the open garden, which was off limits for all of us. I did not think it mattered since I would be leaving the country. It was a feeble, defiant action, but it gave me immense satisfaction. Even though it was still dark, I could make my way to the guava tree. *Mali* and I had raised this tree from a little sapling and named it *Piyari*, meaning "sweetness." In Bangla, guava is called *piyara*; however, in Urdu, the same word, with a slight change in the last vowel, denotes 'sweet' and is generally used as an endearment, such as *piyari ammi*—sweet mom. *Mali* agreed that naming the tree *Piyari* was the most clever and appropriate choice. It was our little secret, which we did not share with other household members. *Mali* and I nurtured *Piyari* and watched her grow tall and strong.

In the dark, I passed my hands over her smooth limbs, remembering the many moments I had climbed all over her, and other times when I curled up against her tall body, eating pink-centered guavas, talking to *Mali*, and watching him tend to the garden. To escape from the rest of the household, I would hide within the petticoat of her leaves and work on my reading assignments. As I traced the knots and fissures on the branches, with my fingers, memorizing all the quirky curves and twists, I wondered whether *Piyari* would miss me climbing all over her, rubbing my face in the perfume of her flowers, to *Mali's* dismay. He would be so afraid that I would bruise them. "No flowers, no guavas, *Choti Bibi*," he would say, and I would laugh, knowing it fully well.

Would *Piyari* miss *Mali* feeding her with tea leaves, dung water, and fruit and vegetable peelings? I was sure she would. And now I will be leaving her as well.

"*Piyari*, you'll be okay. No one will harm you," I said to her quietly. "When the army comes for us, all they have to do is eat one of your guavas, and they will not cut you down or burn you. You'll be safe. Everyone will be safe, I promise you."

A soft sound behind me made me turn around, and Chottubindu stood in the shadows.

"I will take care of *Piyari*," she said, reading my mind.

I don't know how long she stood there. I turned away so she would not see the tears rolling down my face. I held her hand, and together, we visited the rose garden. I pointed out the roses *Abbu* brought from West Pakistan, highlighting the difference between the local roses and the ones *Mali* and I had grafted, naming each one. Next, we went to the jasmine and gardenia section.

"Remember to make a garland of various jasmine flowers for *Ammi* every evening, and don't forget to change the flowers in *Abbu's* vase in their bedroom with fresh tuber roses. You know how he loves those."

I tried not to choke up so that she would not see me cry. I knew that from now on, crying was a private act, and no matter what the situation, I had to resort to my *dou nas laa* training and keep a 'stiff upper lip.' *Abbu* used Kipling's poem *IF* as a standard to develop this character strain in all of us. I started reciting the second-last verse to myself, over and over:

*If you can make a heap of all your winnings*
*And risk it on one turn of pitch-and-toss,*
*And lose, and start again at your beginnings*
*And never breathe a word about your loss;*
*If you can force your heart and nerve and sinew*
*To serve your turn long after they are gone,*
*And so hold on when there is nothing in you*

Hold on, I will, to my family, to my household friends, to the land, to Kaloo, and to all the *piyaris* I was leaving behind. I will hold on to all the Krishnachuras that torch the skies, to the green-carpet paddy fields that extend to eternity, and to the rivers that are as wide as the seas. I will hold on to the lush hills where elephants roam and the young ones eat out of your hands; to the haunting songs of the doyle (magpie robin), the bulbul, and the myna bird; to the cooing of the spotted doves that visit me each morning for their breakfast rice; to the sparkling white sands of Patenga Beach, where I washed my body with the soft clay that the sea bestows on all; and to monsoon-laden clouds that cooled my skin in the hot summers.

I will hold on to all the hopscotch games that Chottubindu and I played with the young girls and boys in the streets of the local markets. I will hold on to the forbidden street food that I enjoy, much to *Ammi's* distress, especially our daily family meals filled with stories and laughter. I will hold on to our yearly Eid festivities, when the entire clan gathered, to the times when we cousins slept in one large space, teasing each other, sneaking out, scaring each other with ghost stories, and basking in the love that permeated throughout the entire household. I will hold on.

# The Encounter

Chittagong (Chattogram), April 15th, 1971. Today is *Pohela Boishak,* the Bangla New Year, 1392, and the 19th day of the Islamic month of Safar. The day of departure neared. I dismissed the thought, for it was a beautiful early dawn. Instead, I decided to visit the burnt Krishnchura groves, half a mile from Octome. Without waking or mentioning my early morning jaunt to anyone, I tiptoed out of Octome and half-ran all the way. It was early, and the smell of charred wood and dew filled the air. I filled my nostrils with the smoky-sweet fragrance of scorched flowers and gently touched the blistered bodies of each tree. Then, on an impulse, I picked up a long stick lying there and started dancing around each tree, tapping them and singing for them to rise from the ashes like a newborn phoenix.

> *Trees of fire, trees of light*
> *Become all phoenix in the night.*
> *Rise, I say, rise and glow,*
> *Turn into beauties that we know.*

As I danced around each tree, chanting my poem and touching one tree while caressing another, I was transported into my little world where the trees began to shake off their blackened garments, rising out of their distorted forms to become red-flowered beauties once more. So absorbed was I in this mirage of my own making when a loud snap of a branch pulled me from my reverie. Turning toward that sound, I locked eyes with a Pakistani soldier who stood behind a large charred Krishnachura tree, his gun pointed in my direction. The song froze in my throat, and I stopped dead in my tracks.

*"Tum Bangal ki jadugarni ho?"* [Are you a Bengali witch?] he asked in Urdu.

*"Gee nahi. Mai to yahhaan ki mahalla me rati houn. Bus mazaa karre thee."* [Oh no! I live around here, and I was just having fun.] I replied in Urdu.

He seemed relieved when I answered in Urdu and not Bangla.

*"Tomare lambe bal aur kale ainkhe se main dargaya. Mai ne Bangal ki jadugarni buhout suna or bola giya hain jo jadugarni dekne ke sati goli karna. Magar tomare Angrazi batou se maien rouk gaiya. Tum Khush naseeb ho jo mai ne goli nahi kara. Tum yahaan akele akale kiyoun ho? Ye Bangal ka jaga hai."*

[Your long hair and dark eyes captivated me. Our mothers have warned us to beware of Bangalee girls like you who seduce young men with witchcraft, and to shoot girls like you the moment our feelings are stirred. You are fortunate! Your singing and dancing in English enchanted me, so I refrained from shooting. Who are you, and what are you doing here? Bangalees reside in this area.]

*"Main to nahi janti, mai to wahaan jati nahi. Main suba aaee serif lakri oothane. Ghar pe lakri nahi hain*

*khana pakane ke liye.*" [I don't know. I came to pick up firewood for cooking since we don't have any at home.]

*"Main tum se pher melunga. Magar ab jaldi chele jaou."* [I will meet you again, but you need to leave right now.] "*Bus jaldi chele jaoun. Koi tum ko bhool se golee chalade ga.*" [Okay, go quickly before someone else sees you and shoots you by mistake.]

*"Buhout shukriya, bhaijaan mai jati houn."* [Thank you very much, dearest brother. I am going immediately.]

Fear and shock gave wings to my feet. I ran further away from Octome until I was sure I was out of the soldier's sight. I turned and took a different narrow street that led me back to the small gardener's entrance into Octome's orchards. I knew I could not enter Octome via the back kitchen door for fear of being noticed. My body shook so hard that my hands couldn't grasp the handle to lift the latch and open the gate.

There, I waited until I stopped shaking and my body returned to normal. Sneaking into my room, I locked the door. My body had gone into shock, and now that I was safely inside, I stood paralyzed, staring at the image of myself in the full-length mirror mounted on the wall.

I looked like a wood nymph with my long, disheveled hair, large eyes, and slender frame wrapped in a long black housecoat that exposed my thin sleeping gown. I did not even recognize this wraith-like figure. Had I lost my senses? I could have, or may have, jeopardized my entire family. I shuddered to think that I had put everyone in Octome at risk.

I recall that my younger *khaloo abba,* who was from

West Pakistan, was told the same by his mother when he informed her that he wished to marry my younger *khala* (mother's younger sister). Mothers of young West Pakistani men often gave this advice before they left for East Pakistan on military tours or jobs so that they would not end up marrying Bengali women.

I pushed my body into the bathroom, turned on the shower, and just stood there, drowning myself under the shower, until a continuous knocking on the bedroom door jerked me back to reality. It was Chottubindu. *"Bibi! Amee dekte ashlaam je gossulkhana te panir sbobdo kano astese?"* asked Chottubindu in Bangla. [I came to check why I heard running water in your bathroom and whether you forgot to turn off the shower since you were not in your room earlier.] Chottubindu always addressed me as *Bibi*.

I turned the shower off, pretended not to hear her, and hurriedly started putting on a set of freshly pressed *shalwar kameez* (loose-fitting trousers that tapered to a tight fit around the ankles, combined with a loose long-sleeve tunic) to join the rest of the family for breakfast. It was eight-thirty, and I had been gone for three hours.

Sadu, our cook, had conjured a special breakfast of *dhoopi pita,* steamed rice cakes stuffed with coconut and goor (molasses). He knew our favorite breakfast food was a specialty of Bengal and that we would not get it in West Pakistan, so I forced a teasing expression to mask my fears of what had happened earlier.

"Sadu, rice cakes for breakfast?" I joked. "You know, once we leave, the government will decrease the rice allowance for our house, so you need to keep the rice for all of you."

Since January, the government has controlled the basic food necessities, which include rice, wheat, tea, sugar, potatoes, lentils, cooking oil, and vegetables. My thoughts flashed back to the afternoon in March when *Ammi* surprised us with small glasses of lime water and a new dessert, which she called tea cakes. She said this was our new teatime custom instead of the usual tea with biscuits (cookies). *Ammi* invented a *petit four* consisting of leftover breakfast tea leaves, finely chopped and combined with palm sugar, cardamom, lemon juice, and rolled in nuts. She wrapped these daintily with rose petals from the garden and secured them with a toothpick.

Even though food supplies were stringent, the food contained *baraka* (divine blessing), and the entire household was grateful for what we received. However, my reminiscing came to a halt when Sadu put a plate of hot, steaming *pitas* in front of me and, with tear-filled eyes, mumbled, "Eat and remember Sadu."

I looked down at my plate. I could not tell him that he was etched into my heart. I could never forget him—all the fun times we had as he showed me how to prepare baked Alaska, plum pudding, chai-spiced bread pudding, and everyone's favorite, chocolate pistachio torte—all of which I bungled each time. How could I forget his feigned irritation?

"Oh, Bibi," he would say. "You think it is so easy! It has taken years to master these dishes, and I cook them on a coal stove and oven with no temperature gauge or timer.

It's called experience! You need to be cooking as long as I have before you can be successful."

I would laugh and say, "Watch next time. I will have it done and give you the day off." I would then leave my mess for him to clean up and skip away while he mumbled that I made work for him each time I came to the kitchen. But I knew he loved my visits.

I will never forget Sadu.

I concentrated on holding back the tears and focusing on the plate of *pitas* before me. I reminded myself: *Live in the present; etch this moment into your memory cells.*

I looked up at my parents' faces for inspiration. They came as refugees from Calcutta to East Pakistan after India was partitioned and made a beautiful life for us in Chittagong. "No looking back," *Abbu* always said.

My parents rarely, if ever, shared stories of their childhood. However, this image of all of us sitting together, eating and talking with our mouths full—Sadu flitting around like a buzzing bee, spoiling us; my brothers grabbing the freshly baked pitas as they come out of the steaming pot; and my *mamoo* and *momani* chatting with their mouths full while praising Sadu's culinary skills—is a memory I want to cherish for the rest of my life.

I was the last to join the group for breakfast, yet no one had questioned me about my whereabouts; I thought that was unusual. There was an unnatural quietness around us—none of the bantering, teasing, or mindless chatter.

Our departure had finally settled into each member's awareness, and while attempts at small talk surfaced from time to time, the atmosphere remained solemn.

All I could think of was the last few sentences of the soldier. I thought to myself that this particular Pakistani soldier wanted to see me again, would come looking for me, and might use that as an excuse to search Octome. I had put the entire household in danger. *Amejan* had always told me that my impulsiveness would get me into big trouble, and I had done it big this time. I had endangered the lives of *Ammi*, *Abbu*, *Khala*, *Khalu*, Chottubindu, and the remaining household members who would remain in Octome after we were gone. I was sick to my stomach and could barely swallow a bite.

"What is wrong? Have I not put enough coconut in it? I put more than usual because you only like coconut and very little *goor*. I used all we had since all specialty items were seized and all food was rationed, so I did my best." Sadu*'s* voice pulled me out of my thoughts.

"Sadu, I'm eating slowly to savor each bite because I know I won't get it again—at least not until I return. So you better stock up on coconut and goor," I said with a forced cheerfulness that even surprised *Abbu*.

"Everything will be okay. Your *khala*, Chottubindu, and I will be all right. Where is your faith?" *Ammi* said quietly.

Startled by her comment, I looked up at her. Why had she said that? Did she know something about my absence from Octome? Yet, if she did, her casual expression gave nothing away.

My relief was mixed with guilt, so I tried to meet everyone's needs. All day, I immersed myself in helping *Mamoo* pack my little cousin's clothes. I engaged in discussions with my younger brothers about what they wanted to take with them, and I stood firm when my youngest brother insisted on taking his stamp collection.

It was the last straw. The new person I was trying to become could no longer tolerate my brother's naivete in believing that we were just going for a lengthy vacation, as our parents had told them.

*Magrib* prayer time was immediately after the sun had set. For as long as I can remember, my brothers and I joined *Abbu* and *Ammi* for the evening prayers. Growing up, this practice allowed us special time with our parents and was one of the many occasions when we learned about the beauty of our faith. It was also the time when *Abbu* blessed each of us with a personal dua.

My brothers and I teased each other about which of us deserved more of Allah Almighty's attention. *Dua* is a conversation with Allah Almighty, in which one asks for protection and all that is good in this life and in the hereafter.

That evening, after prayers, *Abbu* asked me to stay back. Immediately, my guilt overcame me, and I mustered the courage to tell him about what had happened earlier that morning. I wanted to express that he was farsighted and correct, that I should have trusted his and *Ammi's* decision and not resisted them so much. I tried to convey how sorry I was that the army was very close to Octome, and at any moment, they could ransack our home, searching for my brothers, *ChottuBibbi,* and especially me.

"*Abbu,* I—" He interrupted me before I could proceed.

"Please hold your thoughts. I have something important to discuss with you since you will be your brother's guardian starting the day after tomorrow."

What could be more important than what I had to tell him—that I had jeopardized the entire household for the wandering eyes of the Pakistani soldier? But I held my tongue, waiting for him to expose my misadventure. At that very moment, *Ammi* walked in.

"Tomorrow will be a long day and night, and there will be very little sleeping. So I suggest everyone go to bed early and be fresh enough in the morning to remember all the instructions since none will be in writing." He said with a smile. I was glad to be rescued, and as I walked to my room, I could not help but wonder how much *Ammi* knew about my escapade.

# Acquiescence

Chittagong (Chattogram), April 16[th,] 1971. I woke up before Bulbul could chirp his morning wake-up call. I wanted to make this day last and last, not wanting to waste a single minute of it. Dawn conspired with me, holding back her flushed cheeks. There was none of the celadon blue in the typical blue-violet sky. It was still dark, and I slowly made my way through the dim corridors of Octome. Once outside, I noticed that the trees had also collaborated with me, for no leaf moved, despite a soft breeze. I wondered how nature could be so contained and at peace, surrounded by chaos. Dawn's glowing face was slowly bathing the night in light, and the horizon transformed into a gentle line of golden green, uplifting my spirits. I finally understood why *Abbu* had made us memorize Kipling's poem, "IF."

> *If you can meet with Triumph and Disaster*
> *And treat those two impostors just the same,*
> *Or watch the things you gave your life to, broken,*
> *And stoop and build'em with worn-out tools,*
> *Yours is the Earth and everything in it.*

I shall stand up to the adversary, face it directly, and not allow the civil war to pull me down. I would be my brothers' keeper till *Ammi* and *Abbu* join us to build our lives again. I felt energized and did not wait for Bulbul to come and greet me; instead, I greeted Sadu and helped him prepare breakfast. If he was surprised, he did not show it. We both knew it was the last time we would work together and wanted this moment to be etched in our memories. Together, we made *parathas,* layered and puffed tortilla-like flatbreads that are as light and fluffy as French pastry without the glamour and hoop-dee-da. After we cooked them on a hot griddle, I cleaned my station, and if Sadu was surprised, he did not acknowledge. It was the finale of our time together, perfect parathas and a well-trained apprentice, a moment not to be cheapened by pretentious rhetoric.

Soon, the entire family was gathered together, sitting at the table, chatting, smiling, passing the food around, and acting as if it was just another normal day. The atmosphere in the room was highly charged—so much so that if one stuck out their fingers, the electric buzz would course through the whole body. We had all become actors performing a role that could only culminate in tragedy. The young players would exit the scene tomorrow, and the play would continue with four adults. I recognized my parents' sacrifice and felt ashamed that I had only been thinking of myself all this time. It was a dangerous decision they made to sneak us out of the house and send us to Karachi, West Pakistan, under the very noses of the Pakistan Army. I recalled the poem "IF" and decided to contribute to it.

*Life is never broken; life is like a river: It rides through rapids, taking different turns to work its way to smoothness.*

I will be like the river. To my surprise, this thought cheered me up, and I joined my mother, who was busy packing. It was not long before *Abbu* asked me to join him in their bedroom. I anticipated this, so I braced myself to be admonished.

I had a flashback to the many times I had been called to my parents' bedroom. Most of the time, the door would close behind them, and I would be asked to sit. That was when I knew I was in trouble. Other times, they would ask me to sit beside them on the bed, which meant everything was okay and no stern lectures were coming my way. However, this time, it was neither of the two. Instead, *Abbu* asked me to meet him on the balcony adjoining their bedroom, which opened onto the jasmine and tuberose garden. This was a special place where my parents would sit and have tea together. We joined them there occasionally, and only for special events. If I was surprised, I masked it well, for I was puzzled by the gesture of generosity that *Abbu* was showing me.

"Please sit down." He could see that I was confused, so I remained standing. I knew that whatever he had to tell me was not good news, but I was strong enough to face it with fortitude. I thought I caught a hint of a smile on his face, though it might have just been my imagination. *Abbu* wrapped his arms around my shoulders, turning me toward the garden, and in that moment, all my anxiety faded away.

A sense of calm washed over me. The scent of the flowers and *Abbu's* embrace filled me with a surprising composure. I looked at his face and said quietly, "What is it, *Abbu*? You can tell me. I'm not afraid."

"I have arranged with my contacts in Karachi for your brothers to leave for boarding school in England, ensuring their studies are not jeopardized. Mr. Struthers, my business partner in Scotland, will serve as their guardian and take care of everything necessary until your mother and I arrive. I can't share this with your brothers, as it would worry them, but you are old enough and have a steady head on your shoulders."

I thought, *Really, Abbu, do you even know what my steady head has got me into?* But I held my tongue. I could not disappoint him. I would hear him out and then hit him with my encounter with the Pakistani soldier.

"Now, in your case, you have choices: you can either go to England and be with your brothers and attend an art school in London, or you can stay in Karachi and wait for us to travel together to London. Once we arrive, we can decide together about your future, as it wouldn't be practical for you and your mother to return to Chittagong immediately. The other option is to attend art school in the United States, which has offered you a four-year undergraduate scholarship, although it will be challenging for me to cover your living expenses. I have a cousin there who is currently an asylee in the United States, but I can't ask him for financial help."

I felt my legs get weak, and I put my hand out to hold the banister to support myself, all the time not looking up at him. I don't know how long I stood there steadying myself. In the next moment, my legs seemed to have taken on a new role. They became pillars supporting my unsteady body. I felt their strength rising, energizing my back, firming my sternum, and straightening my shoulders. I removed my hands from the banister and stood up tall. My body was strong; I was strong.

"*Abbu*, are you giving me a choice?" I asked in a quiet but firm voice.

"Yes, I am."

"Then I choose to go to the United States. I will go to the land of John F. Kennedy. That's where I can hopefully learn to rebuild a broken country. I can't go to the country responsible for where we are today, a broken nation that should never have been divided in such an outrageous manner. How can a country survive when divided into two parts with an approximate thousand miles of enemy territory bent on ruining us?"

For a split second, *Abbu* was taken aback by my answer. He looked at me, surprised.

"I didn't realize you felt so strongly about the British."

"Not the British, but the British government—the British Raj. First, they colonized us for two hundred years, filling their coffers with our jewels and raw materials. Next, they destroyed our indigenous industries and dumped their second-rate products on us to buy. Not to mention sowing hatred in the hearts of religious communities by pitting one group against another. Not satisfied with that, once they could no longer control us, they were forced to grant us independence, but not before dividing the country into irredeemable regions, fully aware that the two wings of Pakistan could never survive. Hindu India had the Muslims to deal with on two sides, and they controlled us in East Pakistan by surrounding all our borders with their armies, leaving the only unsupervised borders to the unpredictable Bay of Bengal. India had the advantage over Pakistan as they inherited all the major ports of the Indian subcontinent except Karachi and controlled the lifeline of East Pakistan's rivers."

I wanted my father to know that I had chosen the United States because it was a newly formed republic with a history of two hundred years and a mix of diverse cultures, races, and religions. It had also experienced a civil war and managed to reunite itself. Indeed, I could collaborate with a team to help bring our country's two broken wings together. But before I could share all this information to show him that I had done my homework, *Abbu* continued.

"You know nothing about their culture. You will have to relearn how to speak English. Americans don't speak English the way you were taught. Their cultural practices and etiquette differ significantly from what you are accustomed to. You might feel uncomfortable and lonely." But I interrupted him before he could go on.

"I will be a positive 'rolling stone.' I learned English, and I can learn American English. As for their cultural norms, that shouldn't be a problem. You taught us to adapt to any social situation. 'Accommodate yourself to be in the company of the genteel and the everyday worker,' are your words, *Abbu*. I shall accommodate. Right now, I resent being in England, and I don't want to unload my feelings on the people there who had nothing to do with our situation. We find ourselves in this position today because of Churchill and Mountbatten, two racist individuals glorified by the history books. And let's not forget Sir Cyril Radcliffe, who failed to draw a sound geopolitical line delineating and demarcating according to international procedures, pushed by Mountbatten, the true culprit of this unfortunate situation. I also blame Jinnah and Nehru, who, with ambitions to lead their newly formed countries, didn't care to consider the consequences of their actions."

Shocked by this outburst, *Abbu* placed his hands on my shoulder. "Don't be so hard on Jinnah. Initially, he did not include East Pakistan. However, once East Bengal, with its Muslim majority, was designated to Pakistan, he did request a land corridor similar to the Suez Canal agreement when the partition was finalized, which was denied." *Abbu* made excuses for our politicians' blunders, but I was young and unforgiving.

"He should never have agreed because the British couldn't have moved forward without Jinnah accepting the conditions for partitioning India. There would be riots, but since the British took control of India, there have always been riots. Riots in Bengal occurred even before your time, *Abbu*! Didn't it all begin in 1913 when the infamous Lord Curzon separated the eastern parts of Bengal from what was then Bengal proper because its seventy-eight million population was the nerve center of Indian nationalism? It is the British strategy to divide and conquer. They accomplished this by separating the Hindus from the Muslims. They did this throughout their rule in India and again in 1947 to instigate riots. The British carried out similar divisions in all the territories they colonized worldwide, from which neither the lands nor the peoples have ever recovered."

"We must focus on the present. One does not live in the past. Right now, we must decide on what you have expressed. If you are ready to go to the United States, I must consider making that possible."

But I was on a roll.

"I have not forgotten our history, which the British Raj would like us to forget: that Bengal was the most politically and intellectually rich part of undivided India during the Mughal era—"

But *Abbu* gently interrupted me and sat me down in his chair.

"We can talk about this later. Right now, I need you to prepare for tomorrow. Please gather your brothers' school transcripts, promotion documents, and school reports, as we cannot reach the schools immediately. Bring your textbooks so you can continue studying. You will oversee their education to ensure no time is wasted. On the ship, keep all passports separate from your belongings and on your person at all times, and keep them inaccessible to anyone, including your brothers. Remember, from the moment you embark, English must be your language at all times, even in the cabins. The only time you may speak Urdu is when you are with your aunts and cousins. You must not speak Bangla or use any Bangla words whatsoever."

I nodded. There was nothing more to be said. I put myself on automatic.

For the next four hours, I moved like a sleepwalker, completing everything I was asked to do. I did not question; I did not ask anything. I watched motionless as everything I held dear was placed in the two cars that were going with us. I watched but felt nothing. It was as though my heart was put in cold storage. All pretense had subsided; even my little cousin felt something because his constant crying had suddenly died down, and he was quiet. They say that babies are angels who bring calm before the storm. My little cousin was doing his part and not filling the house with his wailing, even though his cries would have been a good excuse for us to vent our anxieties.

Dinner was a simple, quiet affair. Sadu was done. The reality of the situation had finally sunk in, and I felt that he had distanced himself from us as he was never going to see us again. *Yes,* I thought. Sadu had the right idea. This way, it does not hurt as much.

We were to leave for the seaport and board the ship right after *Fajr's* (morning) prayers. We were to rise, get dressed, have breakfast before prayers, and leave while dawn held back her flushed face. No one could sleep. My brothers and I placed some blankets at the foot of my parents' bed so we could be together for the last time. In between instructions, embraces, and moments of silence, *Abbu* would hold us close. Those were moments when nobody spoke; each time it happened, my heart opened to hold it in forever.

*Ammi* never said much; she moved around, busying herself with something or the other until *Abbu* sat her down on the bed next to where he was sitting. I inched my way and sat on the floor between her legs as I always did, and she stroked my hair as always. I felt sheltered and protected, and thought this was how all fetuses feel, nesting in that serene liquid before that safe tank is broken. Is that why the first sound we make is a cry? And now the tank that my parents have created for us cannot hold us anymore either. We must continue our existence in a larger one.

This time, the unpredictable Indian Ocean.

# Part I. The Departure

Chittagong (Chattogram), April 17, 1971. I felt *Ammi's* hands on my shoulders. Had I fallen asleep between her legs? For a moment, I felt disoriented as I realized I was lying at the foot of their bed. How did I get there? *Abbu* must have laid me there. I was upset that they had let me fall asleep.

"You must get ready now," *Ammi* said gently, holding me close to her breast. I stood there, not wanting to remove the shelter that had protected me all my life and which would no longer be reachable. "Take a quick shower, and I mean quick. Your clothes are all pressed and ready for you. Check that you have everything you need on your person, especially your passports. Remember, you are to keep all three passports on your person at all times."

I nodded; I had nothing to say. The Fajr prayer was done, and it was still dark outside. Sadu packed our breakfast and extra food in case we were not served lunch or dinner on the ship. My youngest brother was still half asleep. He was the sleepyhead of the family. I always woke him up for school and dressed him while he slept, standing up. I was glad he would be half asleep this time and not feel the pangs of separation.

I sensed her presence before she said, "We will say our goodbyes here in the bedroom."

That lingering scent of day-old jasmine is embedded in my DNA. For the first time, I felt her bosom tremble as she pressed me to her chest and then immediately left the room. At that moment, it felt as if the life-giving air was no longer in the room, and I gasped for breath. I struggled to breathe and was disoriented. The room spun, and my hands groped for *Ammi's* small frame. Instead, Abbu held me and hugged me in a tight embrace. With his other arm, he gathered my two brothers and walked us to the waiting car. *Mamoo, Momani,* and my cousin were already seated in the blue Consul Cortina and were waiting for us to join them in the green and white Opel Rekord behind theirs. *Abbu* hugged us over and over again. I had to disengage slowly from him because he would not let us go. He had decided to send us away, although now that the time had crept up, he could not face the reality of it all.

I turned slowly, disengaged from his embrace, took my two brothers by the hand, and walked to the car. My middle brother walked to the front seat, and my youngest got in the back, too sleepy to argue for the front seat. As I got in the car, I turned to look at *Abbu* for the last time and felt my heart burst. His handsome face had aged, and for the first time, I saw how separating from us affected him. He stood there, his usually upright, straight shoulders stooped, his face gaunt with sadness. I told the chauffeur to stop the car, and I jumped out and ran to him.

"*Abbu*, it's going to be okay. You know I'll take care of the boys, and I can take care of myself. I'll be fine; I'm strong. I'm like *Ammi*, right?"

He forced a smile. "She says that you are like me."

"Maybe I am half you and half her."

But I could see that the sudden wave of loss reflected on his face had disappeared for the moment. I knew it would return once we were gone, but *Ammi* would know how to handle it.

The car moved slowly out of the driveway, and as I turned for a last look at Octome, my eyes immediately went to my parents' bedroom balcony, where Ammi stood, her small frame swallowed by Octome. She looked so tiny and vulnerable that my heart pounded fiercely against my ribs as if it would break free from the cage imprisoning it and fly out to her. At that moment, I became her mother. I wanted to comfort her, to stop the car, run back, and tell her not to be afraid, that I could handle the entire world—hadn't I faced the Pakistani soldier? Instead, I closed my eyes and sent my thoughts to her. I was confident she would receive them. In that instant, a sense of peace washed over me. I released the tight grip on my youngest brother's hand and glanced over to see if he had noticed that I had clenched his hand hard enough to turn it white. If he felt it, he didn't acknowledge it. He was trying so hard to be a big boy and not cry that I hugged him, and in that moment, my future role flashed before my eyes. I was not just their guardian; I was their Mum until *Ammi* could take over again, and I would do anything to keep them safe.

As the car moved slowly past the charred grove of Krishnachura trees, all I could see was a burnt, devastated land—a far cry from 'The Eastern Land of the Pure'—East Pakistan, rather a place tainted with the blood of its people.

I choked on sheer nothingness. I tried to recall the sweet scent of the gardenias, but my memory was on strike, and all I could inhale was the musty, damp stench of the blistered Krishnachuras in the distance. All the dreams I had came crashing down, singed to ashes. As my thoughts turned to carbon, I remembered the song I had sung to the Krishnachura trees, and by changing the last two lines of the song, I softly repeated it under my breath.

*'Rise, I say, rise and Be*
*Become the person you want to see.'*

Surprisingly, this newly formed mantra gave me courage and hope. Is this how *Abbu* and *Ammi* felt when they left Calcutta for East Pakistan, leaving all their childhood memories, friends, and familiar places? They made a new life for themselves in a new country, and I was to do the same. History repeats itself, and I have *Ammi* and *Abbu* to show me the way. Going to America is as illogical as their leaving Calcutta. They survived, and I would too. I would not worry about my finances, at least not for now. I must ride Destiny's chariot, for it will take me where I need to go. Going to America is where my colonized socio-identity will remake itself. There, I will learn to restore my true identity and heritage. I told my brain to stop overthinking, calm itself, and stop racing ahead.

Just as I was getting accustomed to this new turn in my life, the car braked, coming to a complete stop, and there in front of us was a herd of army heads and bodies surrounding *Mamoo's* Cortina. Almost immediately, I told my youngest brother to climb down into the footwell of the back seat, instructing him not to move or make a sound as I covered him with pillows and blankets and waited. We saw *Momani* come out of the car speaking Punjabi excitedly, which captivated the Pakistani soldiers who were not expecting a vivacious redhead with large painted eyes and flawless skin, waving her hand and showing her frustration at being stopped. She had a flair for dramatics and was making the most of it. I could see her pointing to our car, and between her exaggerated gestures and loud laughter, the soldiers were quite captivated. *Momani* was loud, fun-loving, and loved to perform. She was making the most of the situation and had the soldiers eating out of her hand—a stark contrast to my encounter with the Pakistani soldier!

My youngest *Momani* was different from all my *Khalas* (mother's sisters) and my older Momani, who was quite prim and very proper. From the car's back seat, all I could see were her hands flying about and snippets of her excited voice. I could not make out what was being said. In an excited and loud voice, she pointed to our car, which made the soldiers look in our direction. I thought to myself, what was she telling them? I hope she is not overdoing her theatrics! In the meantime, I could hear my brother's muffled voice, wanting to know when he could ditch all the pillows and blankets and come up. I told him to stay where he was until I gave him the okay signal. The few moments that felt like hours finally ended, and I saw *Momani* climb back into the car. The soldiers motioned us to continue driving. To my surprise, we were escorted by a fleet of military jeeps.

I told my brother that the coast was clear and that he could come out of his hiding place. It was not soon enough for him, and he let me know by his belligerent behavior. I just ignored him, trying hard to act mature. As I looked out of the window, I watched us drive through the famous Tiger Pass, a narrow two-mile road that cut through a forest of Shimul, Sundari, and Mahogany trees, said to be the nesting place of the Royal Bengal tigers before British days. I waved a small goodbye to Batali Hills. My eyes searched out the winding snake-like road that went to the top of the Hills, where each year we gathered to sight the new moon on the 29th evening of Ramadan (the 9th month of the Islamic calendar and the month of fasting), hoping that the festival of Eid would follow the next day. I thought of our clan get-togethers and all the shenanigans, and I promised myself that they would not be memories but my box of treasures to open whenever I desired. The thought cheered me. Nothing is lost if the mind can bring back to life, past experiences.

As the car drove over the railroad tracks to get onto the Agrabad road leading us to the harbor where the ship was docked, we slowed and stopped right in front of my older *mamoo's* office building. On Saturday mornings, we would pick him up from his office and drive to Patenga Beach, where we would swim, play in the sand, and have cucumber sandwiches with hot tea. *Mamoo's* office had built a cottage on the beach, and he loved to take us there. It was our special time together. We would build bonfires with driftwood that I gathered from around the shore, and

*Mamoo* would tell us stories from his days as the leader of the Jamboree Scouts, especially his trips to Australia. Invariably, we would end up singing the Kookaburra song.

*Kookaburra sits on the old gum tree*
*Merry, merry king of the bush is he*
*Laugh, Kookaburra laugh*
*Kookaburra gay your life must be*
*Kookaburra sits on the old gum tree*
*Eating all the gumdrops he can see*
*Stop...*

"Stop, *Apa*. Why are you singing this song?" cried my younger brother. I did not realize I was singing the song aloud. I squeezed his hand, stopped singing, and let my thoughts return to the beach. This time, my daydreaming was more deliberate.

I was back on the sands of Patenga beach, watching my *mamoo* and brother swim while I drew on the sand. The waves were transforming my drawings into unique patterns, and I was conversing with them, drawing over the washed-out lines. The gentle morning light was my accomplice, edging me to draw faster before the waves returned to wash them out. I worked quickly to create a rhythm, redrawing my original drawing before the waves thrashed back to erase it. We had an unspoken understanding and shared respect; like always, the ocean had the last say. My daydreaming had brought me a message. It is okay to lose. Losing allows you to build something new.

I felt energized. I hugged my brother, who squirmed and gently disengaged himself to point excitedly to a ship in the distance. We had arrived at one of the banks of the Karnaphuli River. We watched as the army cars guided us to a long stretch of road that led to where the ship was docked, and watched them drive away. The road ran parallel to the river, and we could see the sky-blue shape of the vessel in the distance. The initial excitement of seeing the ship gave way to a sudden feeling of anxiety, and I could feel the tension that my brothers were experiencing.

"Do you remember when we took the launch (houseboat) up the Karnaphuli River? A pod of dolphins was swimming alongside the launch, and both of you jumped in before we could stop you?"

I was trying hard to distract my brothers from the inevitable that would happen soon.

"Oh yes, all of you were shouting for the launch master to stop the launch. There was so much panic, and *Ammi* was so upset, but it was also a lot of fun, even though we received the scolding of our lives. But we'll never do that again, so why talk about that?"

My youngest brother, the pragmatist, never failed to bring us back to reality.

"The memories of swimming with them will carry you wherever you go. Your experiences are never lost. They are etched into your genes for you to indulge in them wherever you may be," I said to him, although by speaking the words out loud, I was consoling my aching heart.

"Why don't you change places with me and sit near

the window? Perhaps you will see the dolphins as we drive along the Karnaphuli," I told my youngest brother.

"It's a long drive to the ship, and since it is early morning, there is a chance we might see dolphins on our way. You can wave at them."

"But don't you think we are too close to the sea? River dolphins don't venture so close to the sea; the sharks are their nemesis, and the Bay is full of sharks. These dolphins are not like their sea cousins. They are practically blind as their eyes are tiny, and they swim totally by sound vibrations."

"Oh? I didn't know that!"

I pretended not to know and smiled. My youngest brother, our mad scientist, was quick to point out that I was misinformed. But I had done my job. I had distracted both of them. They rolled down the windows and stuck their heads out to look for dolphins, easing the tense atmosphere in the car.

I, too, turned my gaze toward the river as it grew wider and wider, changing color from brilliant blue-green to terracotta, making its way to the mouth of the Bay of Bengal. I kept my eyes glued on the rhythm of the waves as one wave turned into another, slowly changing its pace to harmonize with those of the sea. I remembered a verse in the Quran: *It is God who has caused two bodies of water to flow, one palpable and sweet, the other salty and bitter. Placing between them a barrier they cannot cross.* (Quran, Al-Furqan, The Criterion, Chapter 25: Verse 53). As I recited the verse repeatedly, I felt a calm prevail in the car's atmosphere.

A wave of serenity washed over us as the car gradually stopped in front of the pier's makeshift gangway. The calm brought a surge of recognition. I envisioned myself as the river moving forth to meet the sea of my destiny. A new wave of empowerment flowed through me, starting in my gut and reaching my fingertips. It felt like a tune tingling the very nerves of my hair follicles. In the Quran, I interpreted the word 'barrier' as my place of interlude, a physical and emotional space where I would undergo a total metamorphosis.

The car stopped a few yards from the ship's makeshift gangway. A crowd of pro-Pakistani Bengali haters waited to embark and flee from what they anticipated would be an impending doom striking the already blood-soaked country of East Pakistan. However, *Momani's* brother, an admiral in the Pakistan Navy, was there to greet us, and we were quickly ushered aboard the ship.

I decided that all three of us would board the ship together. With my head held high, I took each of my brothers by the hand and walked up the gangway. As I walked, my eyes went to the starboard side of the ship, and there in very bold letters was the name *Shams*—the sun in Arabic. I felt my entire vision encircled by the name of the vessel. It was a sign. We were meant to sail on *Shams,* the star providing energy and healing. A flood of images surged within me, starting with the blue-green river, the guiding star, and the chilling cerulean blue waters of the Bay of Bengal.

I recognized these signs displayed throughout the entire car ride. I no longer felt vulnerable. Each of us received a barrier for our protection. For my brothers and me, it represented our *dou nas laa* identity—our invisible shield that would keep us safe amid the sea of Pakistani nationalists.

Like the river, I was ready to meet my *sea*.

# Part II. The Shams

I stepped onto the deck of *Shams* and sang the third verse of Nazrul's 1928 poem very softly under my breath repeatedly as we followed the admiral to our cabin.

| *Nôbô nôbiner gahiya gan* | *The youngest of the young, will sing a song;* |
|---|---|
| *Sôjib kôribô môhashôshman* | *From buried bones, we will raise the living;* |
| *Amra danibô nôtun pran* | *And we will be the ones to give them new life* |
| *Bahute nôbin bôl…* | *With the might of our new arm…* |
| *Chôl re Chôl re Chôl* | *March and March, and March* |
| *Chôl Chôl Chôl* | *March March March* |

"There is nothing to fear," he said. "Everyone has been informed that you are my family members returning to Karachi with my sister and her husband. You can explore the ship, so feel free to make it your home for the next seven days. The ship will first stop at the Port of Molang in Khulna to pick up passengers, some of whom have lost family members. I recommend staying in your cabin the entire time we are docked there. Our next stop will be Colombo for refueling, as India is at war with us. Although Ceylon (Sri Lanka) is a friendly country and you can disembark, I suggest remaining on the ship. After that, it is a three-day journey to Karachi."

The kindness in the admiral's voice made it difficult for me to check the tears welling up in my eyes. I could only nod, afraid to speak in case my voice trembled.

"You can release their hands," he said softly.

I was surprised to find that I was still holding onto the hands of both my brothers, and even more amazed that they had let me do so. I let go of their hands abruptly, embarrassed that I had subjected them to my insecurities.

The door to our cabin was on the right side of a long, rectilinear-shaped compartment. It was a generous space. Two sets of bunker beds faced each other, separated by a dresser. The dresser had a built-in leaf that pulled out to form a decent-sized study table. Two chairs with padded seats were on either side of the dresser. At the opposite end was an alcove with a built-in closet, a small changing space, and a complete washroom. Our luggage was stacked neatly in the alcove, waiting for us to hang some of our clothes for the seven-day journey. The admiral had thought of everything.

"Is everything suitable, and is the room big enough?" he asked in Urdu.

"Yes, Admiral, you've considered everything. We will be very comfortable, thank you," I replied in English.

He turned to face me and said gently, "You can put your guard down. You'll be protected here on the ship whenever and wherever you roam. I have given instructions to the whole crew so you can be yourselves. You're safe."

With tear-filled eyes, I nodded, too emotional to speak. I couldn't reveal *Abbu's* instructions to always speak English. Besides, I had never ventured out on my own, nor had I managed money. *Ammi* took care of all my needs. She designed and tailor-stitched my clothes. Even my newfound interest in painting was made possible by her. She purchased the paints, brushes, and painting boards cut to the desired sizes. Together, we would go to the framing shop and have them framed—some of which she gifted to friends, while others were auctioned to raise money for her school for low-income children. I was content to live under my mother's shelter.

Being suddenly placed in charge of the safety and well-being of my brothers, only able to speak English instead of our family's language, *and* being on guard at all times was a tall order from my parents. What if I slipped? We were fleeing from those who were taking us to safety. It was comical, if not tragic. The civil war tearing the country apart had nothing to do with language or ethnicity. It was all about a military regime unwilling to relinquish power and using whatever means necessary to divide, conquer, and force submission, just as they had historically done in Pakistan. My pent-up apprehension gave way to unsettling anger.

I was angry because, like so many of my generation, we were repeatedly told, both at home and in school, that we were privileged. We were the rising players in a new, free country—Pakistan—unshackled from the chains of colonization. We emerged from the dust of the past to achieve extraordinary things. I felt privileged; I was privileged. Yet, now I was fleeing from the people who were supposed to protect us and help us realize our destiny in this beautiful new country. Most of the individuals the army had massacred were young people, primarily students—the future of our country. It didn't make sense to me. All these thoughts swirled within me like raging, wind-driven monsoon clouds.

I recalled that *Ammi* had repeatedly impressed us with the importance of learning impeccable Urdu and Bangla languages, yet I had failed to do so. I had neglected to know about my own cultural identity. I had been unable to refine, dream, and build myself in the culture for which the country was created. Instead, I had taken the easy way out by continuing to perfect what I was already practicing seven hours a day in school. The blame rested entirely on my shoulders. My brothers and I were sent to private, parochial schools, taught by British people of cloth and groomed in the English language, British culture, history, and the arts. I, in particular, had done nothing to educate myself about my heritage.

Although we spoke to our parents in Urdu and studied Bangla as a second language, the rest fell through the cracks. There was just not enough time in the day—and, more importantly, a lack of interest in exploring the full scope of our cultural identity. We took an unspoken pride in interacting with our peers in the language of the poets, musicians, writers, and historians we studied and admired, forsaking our cultural and religious identity.

We were unconsciously grooming ourselves to become what Lord Thomas Macaulay wanted for the Indian subcontinent: a class of people. 'Indian in blood and color, but English in taste, opinions, morals, and intellect.' Right in front of *Amejan's* eyes, we were growing up as *dou nas las,* erasing our ethnic and religious identities.

A wave of shame hit me like a savage tsunami, drowning me in loneliness and humiliation.

I must have blacked out, either from sadness or shame. When I opened my eyes, I saw that I was lying on one of the lower bunker beds. My shoes were removed, and a pillow was under my head. *Mamoo*, a man of few words, had summed up my physical state.

"She's emotionally exhausted. All this responsibility has been too much for her young shoulders. Let her rest. We'll go to lunch and bring her a plate of food."

Relieved, I kept my eyes closed and lay still, waiting for everyone to leave. I needed some quiet time to process everything that had led us to this final situation. Once I heard everyone depart and the door lock from the outside, I huddled under the sheets, pulling my knees up to my hips to form a human ball to warm my shivering body. I focused my thoughts on *Ammi* and *Abbu* to steady myself.

I told myself that I had let my parents down. Their generation was deeply rooted in their language and cultural history, and the British had not entirely severed them from their cultural identity. They were, to a certain extent, brainwashed to believe that their children would be prepared for the new world of science and technology by not only adopting Western education but also the culture and customs.

My parents, like all other parents, had forgotten that Muslims embrace knowledge from all cultural sources without sacrificing their cultural identities. My parents were part of one of the largest migrations in modern history, comprising men, women, children, and animals. I was told that during the partition of India, millions lost their lives, and around fourteen million were displaced, with our family being one of them. Both of my parents' families felt the impact of this evacuation. They were given less than a day to leave Calcutta, their ancestral home and the home of millions of Muslims.

In newly formed Pakistan, my parents were part of the new order of the country, still under the whip of their colonial masters, unconsciously fulfilling the dream of Sir Macauley. So here we were, children with a partial cultural memory. As I lay there, drifting in and out of consciousness, I told myself I could either be a victim or change my situation. No matter what I studied or did in the United States, I would dedicate myself to filling this deep cultural void that gnawed on my ancestral memory, leaving me without answers.

I must have fallen into a deep sleep for quite a while. When my eyes opened, I saw a plate of food on a stool close to my bed and voices outside the cabin door. I jumped up. It was five o'clock in the afternoon. I had slept for six hours. The door opened, and my brothers came running in.

"*Apa*, we are leaving Chittagong," they cried in

unison. "You are going to miss saying goodbye."

I grabbed my shawl and wrapped it around me tightly, for suddenly, I felt a clammy chill pass through my entire body. It started with my feet getting heavy and cold and the chill's icy hands slowly grabbing my thighs and reaching for my stomach. I was frozen to the ground, unable to move. My youngest brother looked at me, perplexed; he couldn't understand why I was not moving. He just shook his head, exasperated, grabbed my hand, and dragged me out of the cabin to the ship's starboard that faced the dock.

*Shams* was slowly and graciously gliding out to sea from the concrete dock where she was anchored. She was giving her cargo and passengers all the time to say their goodbyes.

Crowds of people left their cabins and rushed to the ship's starboard; some climbed on top of the cargo *Shams* was carrying back to Karachi to bid goodbye to what they were leaving behind. Some showed their fists, others raised their hands in supplication, thankful that they were escaping, while others shouted curses out aloud at Bengalis in general, damning the country that they were leaving behind. Many sang the Pakistan national anthem.

These East Pakistanis had never seen themselves as part of the Bengali population. They were Urdu-speaking migrants from the 1947 partitioned India, and who saw themselves as superior to the indigenous people of the land to which they had migrated. In the twenty-three years they had lived in East Pakistan, they had never deemed it necessary to learn Bengali (Bangla), the language of East

Pakistan, or connect with the locals. They judged themselves superior to the Bengalis and turned their loyalty toward their Urdu-speaking migrant communities and to the army, which was comprised mainly of West Pakistanis.

Unfortunately, many of them suffered cruelty at the hands of local Bengali mobs after the first massacre of Bengali students, academics, and businessmen by the Pakistan Army.

Amidst all this commotion, I felt totally out of place, and a sudden surge of nausea filled my throat, and I gasped for breath. I must have turned pale because *Mamoo*, who had been watching, was immediately by my side.

"I think you should get away from the crowd. You're feeling lightheaded because you haven't eaten all day. If you like, you can escape the crowd by going to the ship's port(left) side."

I nodded—anything to get away from the madding crowd.

"Will you keep a tight eye on the boys, *Mamoo*? I don't want them to miss out on getting a last glimpse of Chittagong. I feel suffocated among this crowd."

"They will be right beside me. Just go. You're just on the other side of the ship, and if they want to join you, I will bring them over."

Grateful to escape, I crossed over to the port and made my way up to the bow of *Shams*.

Looking at the view from this side of the ship, I turned my gaze back at the Karnaphuli River as she snaked her way reluctantly to join the sea. Her beautiful body was already changing from turquoise blue to deep green. I strained my eyes to see as far as I could so that I could imprint her sinuous form into my DNA.

I watched the river dolphins swim alongside the ship, whistling and clicking. When one of them swam close, I bent over the deck railing and shouted, "Remember me, for I will remember you." I knew they would go as far as the river would allow them. Once the waters mixed with the sea, they would turn back. I willed their faces onto the walls of my heart so that the imprints would remain forever and I would never lose them.

As *Shams* gathered more speed, the dolphins stayed back, and the color of the waters began to shift to a mottled green. I moved my attention to the landmasses on either side of *Shams*. They were both quite different. The land on my left glistened in the sun like a sparkling emerald and stretched all the way my eyes could see. This green, unspoiled terrain was the district of Patiya. The green paddy fields close to the shoreline swayed gently in the breeze, and I remembered my third khala referring to the paddy fields as the green carpet of East Pakistan. Greenery, nature's comforter, can soothe our eyes and calm our emotions, and I was lulled.

It was seemingly quiet on this side of the isthmus. Nothing moved except *Shams* and the waves. There was no sign of human habitation, even though one could always see villages close to the mouth of the rivers, with people swimming and fishing. *Shams* glided softly, smoothly over the calm, final waters of the Karnaphuli. It was as though she was stealing her way out of the chaos, leaving behind the blood-soaked city of Chittagong. Patenga Beach held many of my happiest childhood memories and appeared almost as a sandy line on my right.

I turned my eyes to the waves forming and dying simultaneously as *Shams* sliced through them, cutting them into shreds. The waters were changing from a transparent turquoise to a somewhat dull sap green, turning an unusual color on entering the waters of the 'barrier.' What happens to the waters of the river as they merge with the waters of the sea? Do they dominate, fight, and submit? The Quran states: *"And Allah it is who has joined the two seas; one sweet and palatable and the other saltish and bitter; and placed between them a barrier"* (25:53). What is the Quran asking us to do—ponder, analyze, and learn? What novelty is to be found in this deep expanse of water where the two meet? What kind of sea vegetation grows on the seafloor? Do new creatures develop specific to these waters? How do they survive in a sweet and saline environment?

Why am I sailing through this barrier? Like all the rest of my extended family members, I could have flown to West Pakistan. Yet here I am, navigating the barrier's calm and murky waters, being teased to find the secrets of survival and continuity. I felt my head reeling with questions to which I had no answers. My legs felt weak, and I grabbed the railing tightly with both hands to steady myself on the deck.

*"Baji, aap bohaut khatarnak jagey me kharee hain. Zara maherbani se hutt jaiya? Samundar bouhat beegar raha he."* [Sister, you are dangerously close to the railing;

please step away. The sea is starting to get angry.]

My hands froze on the railing, for I recognized that voice. For a split second, I did not know whether I should turn around or stay where I was. I stood still and prayed for intervention. Relief did come in the form of the second captain.

"*Sipahi, tum yahaan kiya kar rahe ho? Ye captan sahib ki bhangee hai. Bus apne kam pe chale jaaeen.*" [Soldier, what are you doing here? This is the captain's ward, and she has permission to be on any part of this ship. Please return to your duties.]

Upon hearing another voice, I turned around and stared into the eyes of the young soldier who had witnessed my eccentric early-morning dance amidst the Krishnachura trees. Although I recognized him, I showed no sign of it. I could see that he was confused. I looked him square in the face, turned my gaze to the chief officer, and spoke quietly in English.

"I'm sorry; I didn't mean to trouble you. I felt overwhelmed by the crowd, so I came here for some fresh air. Is there a problem?"

"Not at all, Miss. Please be careful as you are at the bow of the ship. We are heading out into the ocean very soon and will experience swells that will cause extreme wave turbulence. Please excuse the soldier; he was only concerned about your welfare."

Relieved that the soldier was gone, I thanked the officer and told him I would be careful and leave shortly. I turned away from him, feeling secure. I told myself that if the soldier recognized me, he would either think he was mistaken or lack the courage to approach me or challenge me regarding my presence that ill-fated morning at the Krishnachura groves, miles from our home.

Feeling confident and empowered, I moved toward the furthest nose of *Shams* and pretended to be her figurehead, her protector. Standing precariously at the ship's bow, I took in the panoramic view of the sea flanked by the two shorelines and the endless Indian Ocean. I stood on the deck and turned to rest my eyes on every little part of the land I was leaving behind. Patiya had turned into a green shape, and Patanga Beach's shoreline was barely visible. My face was wet, but not from tears. The high waves slammed the bow, drenching the ship's deck as *Shams* ripped her way out to sea, desperate to leave the bloody turmoil of the land of Chittagong. All at once, the darkness that had captured my mind dissipated, and I heard a voice rise from the waters.

*Be like the waters of the ocean. We surround all continents yet belong to none. We cannot be contained. We flow unconfined. We simply flow. Learn to flow.*

Finally, I understood. Like water that flows, floods, and freezes yet remains water, I, too, stripped, stretched, sore, and saddened—I stay the credulous girl from the beaches of Chittagong. As I basked in this new revelation, I felt the presence of my brothers on either side of me, their hands slipping into mine. Silently, we watched the sun begin to set on the horizon. Soon, it would be *Magrib*, the time for the fourth prayer of the day. This was a congregational prayer led by *Abbu* in our home. It was the time of day when all work and play were set aside, and we, as a family, thanked the Great Protector for all that we enjoyed. *Abbu* always ended the evening with a special prayer for us, taking our faces in his hands and blowing the *dua* (blessings) onto our foreheads. An abrupt heave caused by *Shams*'s sudden change of direction broke my chain of thoughts, and I grabbed each of my brothers by their hands.

"Hold on to the rail with your other hand," I shouted, "*Shams* is turning to the right."

"Yes, but look, *Apa*," shouted my youngest brother, caught in the euphoria of the dramatic speed change. "The sun has cast a golden bridge for us, and *Shams* has altered her course by turning right to sail on it."

The sun had lengthened into a glistening ladder, encouraging *Shams* and us to coast on its golden energy.

"*Apa*, look, we have all turned gold, even the ship."

I looked at us and then around, and sure enough, we were all enveloped in the yellow-golden light that bathed us, the deck, and the walls of the Captain's Bridge. I had never seen my brothers so excited. The last time I encountered them this happy was when *Abbu* returned home from the Chittagong Circuit House killing fields. Gazing at their joyful faces, I was filled with a profound sense of gratitude. We were together; we were alive. This golden orb enveloped us in warmth, reminding me that *Ammi* is with us each day, no matter where we are. It is only fitting that we should sail into the sun, for my mother embodied it. She is a healer, comforter, nurturer, and nourisher, guiding us through all that transpired. I smiled, feeling a soothing assurance rise within me. I gently let go of my brothers' hands, then lifted my own toward the horizon to catch the fading sun with outstretched arms.